STOLEN ROADS

STOLEN ROADS

RANDY CHANDLER

RED ROOM PRESS

PROLOGUE

The boy crawls from the wreckage and slithers, blood-slimed, through tall grass and onto soft earth. He isn't sure what happened but he's certain that something like it has happened before—that he slid into a strange world sheathed in a slick glaze of his mother's blood, struggling for breath and for light.

The only light now is the light he holds in his memory. He remembers the moon and the way it sank into an angry ocean of darkness. He watched through the windshield as it became little more than a luminescent smudge and then finally disappeared behind scudding rain clouds. He was sitting on the seat between them, mother and father. His hand went up to touch the cool glass where the moon had been and his mother said, "What is it, hon?"

And his father said, "You know what it is. He's not ready. They released him too soon."

His mother's hand turned moon-white on the steering wheel but she never had the chance to challenge his father's assertion. She shrieked and the car swerved wildly, left the curving road, crashed through a guardrail and plunged down a steep embankment, into subterranean darkness.

The grass is wet and cool, but he doesn't know if it's dew or his mother's cooling blood he feels on his arms and face. His father is no longer there. The passenger's seat is empty and the windshield sports a jagged hole with an areola of crystalline facets, so he supposes that his father catapulted through it and must be out there in the weeds. Almost certainly dead. As is his mother, crushed by the steering wheel. Odd that the airbags didn't deploy.

Lightning bestows a stingy measure of illumination. He sees his father's body asprawl at the foot of a tall tree. He hears a deep moan followed by a forlorn mewling sound coming from his father's throat. He crawls toward him. Spindly grass tickles his face and arms. The earth gives up a graveyard scent.

Next flash of lightning reveals the otherworldly thing crouched on his father's chest.

The boy stops, balanced precariously on his hands and knees, and tries to make sense of the thing he has just seen in the lightning. But nothing in his mental inventory of the planet's natural creatures jibes with this pebble-skinned thing nearly as big as a man, a terrifying thing with spiky shoulders and lizard-like snout, its long knobby limbs folded insect fashion as if it might suddenly leap or fly away without warning.

He wants to crawl forward but his arms and legs are trembling too violently, expressing the fear his mind refuses to recognize, because after all, the thing he thinks he saw could not be real. He has seen such things before, phantasms and mythological creatures deemed hallucinations by men in white coats, by esteemed doctors of the mind. The medication is supposed to stop him from seeing such forbidden sights. And yet this thing is somehow different, more solidly in the world than any hallucination could ever be. Surely this thing *is* real. And it is doing something terrible to his broken father.

A long train of thunder rumbles behind the boy, as if a phantom convoy is rolling along the paved road above, on its way to soggy oblivion.

He hears the awful gurgling sound from his father's throat, followed by deep silence, and he thinks his father must be dead.

The words blurt out of the boy of their own accord: "Get off my dad!"

Another flash of lightning paints the creature with whitish luminescence as it unlimbers its long appendages and starts toward the boy. Its eyes shine red.

Now his mind does register fear. He is afraid the thing will steal his life from him the same way it took the last of his father's.

The creature comes on through the darkness, its flashing eyes still holding fire from the last spangle of lightning. The boy falls back on his haunches, a scream stuck in his throat.

The thing touches him, gently at first. Then it rakes a claw down his left cheek and hooks it under his eye, flicking loose a flap of flesh, drawing blood. The boy smells ozone and an underlying scent unlike anything he's ever smelled. His scalp tingles.

Lightning strikes the tall tree towering over the boy's father and a blinding ball of white electricity explodes in a shower of sparks like a fireworks display gone astray.

The creature leans down and puts its snout in the boy's face, as if taking his scent. It makes sibilant snuffling sounds, and then its wet spongy tongue flicks out to lash the wound on the boy's cheek. Its saliva burns like acid.

The creature withdraws into darkness. Gone.

Now the rain comes. On his back in the grass, the boy shivers in shock, chilled by the merciless downpour. The blanket of darkness offers no warmth.

Later, he slips and slides up the embankment and stands for a time at the side of the road. The rain has ended and the moon resurfaces overhead, hoary and cold.

The road is a silvered river emptying into a dark ocean of deep night.

CHAPTER 1

He swung down from the shuddering rig, threw a salute to the truck driver, and sauntered across the gravel parking lot, the scarlet sunset at his back. He paused in front of the Hoot'n'Holler to admire the way the sinking sun painted the roadhouse a fairytale red, then he stepped inside and headed for the long oak bar.

Rita watched him come, boldly admiring his long-legged stride and the easy moves of his lanky frame. His red-and-black checkered flannel shirt fitted him loosely. His jeans were as tight as a skin-diver's wetsuit. His straw-colored hair hung to his shoulders, and he sported a mustache with long droopy handles like the one Wild Bill Hickok had favored in his latter days.

"Home is the sailor," she said, waving her bar rag like a small soggy flag, "from the asphalt sea."

He doffed his faded ballcap, shrugged out of his backpack and climbed onto a barstool.

"Long time, Kidd," she said as she drew him a mug of draught and set it in front of him.

"Really? Doesn't seem that way to me," he said. "Deep maybe, but not that long."

Rita turned and took the calendar off the wall behind the cash register and brought it back to the bar. She flipped back through September and August. "I marked it on the calendar," she said. "You didn't know I keep track of your comings and goings?"

"No, I didn't," he said, his mustache bracketing a frown. "Why would you do that?"

She tapped a blocked number with her stubby fingernail. "Right there it is. August twenty-third. What's that say?"

He read it upside-down: "'Kidd lights out.' But why?"

She pulled a pen from behind her ear and in the square for October 25 she wrote "Kidd returns."

He tipped the mug and slurped a sip of foamy brew. "Say."

Rita wiped a spot on the bar that didn't need wiping. "Coz I ain't figured you out yet. Everybody else comes in here—the regulars, I mean—I got figured. Hell, it ain't that hard. But you..." She shook her head. "You're a mystery. Maybe even a mystery unto yourself. I won't say you don't know if you're coming or going, but that might be the only thing you do know for sure. So, I figure if I track your movements long enough a pattern might emerge and give some clue as to just what in hell you're really up to."

Kidd grinned. "My *movements* aren't on your calendar. But this shit...?" He shook his head and let the grin drop.

She swatted him with the bar rag. "Get your mind outta the outhouse, Kidd. I run a respectable joint here."

"With an iron fist. In a velvet glove."

Rita laughed. It was a deep, boisterous laugh that came up from her flat belly, shook her modest allotment of bosom and put sparkles in her eyes. It was a laugh that sounded too big to come out of such a slender woman. Kidd figured it came from the deep well of her heart.

She popped open the cash register drawer and pulled out what looked like a business card. "Before I forget," she said, waving the card under his nose, "a man left this for you last week."

Kidd took the card and read it. He absently traced a fingertip along the crescent-shaped scar under his left eye.

George and Mallory Flucker, Fantastic Investigators
"Lost roads are our specialty."
New Orleans, LA   naked2lunch@gmail.com

"Huh," he said and stared at the card as if a secret message might suddenly appear.

"Flip it over. There's a note on the back."

He flipped the card and read the blue-inked script on the back: "We need your help. We know you what you have seen." *Seen* was underlined twice. Printed beneath this improbable message was a phone number.

"What'd the guy look like?" He tapped the edge of the card on the bar.

"Like a priest on the sauce," said Rita, shrugging. "Auburn beard, bushy eyebrows, ruddy complexion. A little on the chubby side. Nice looking gentleman. Ring a bell?"

"No." He stared blankly at the card. Turned it back over. Tapped its edge again.

"You have no idea who he is?" Rita shot him a skeptical look.

"No clue."

"They know what you've seen?" She shook her head, perplexed.

"I don't know them but they must know me. My…shady history."

"Your psych history?"

He nodded and took another pull from his mug of beer, then wiped foam from his mustache with the back of his hand. "So somebody told them about me."

"Who would do that? You know I wouldn't."

"I know that." He stared at the e-mail address. *naked2lunch*. The Fluckers, George and Mallory, had obviously taken their e-mail moniker from *Naked Lunch*, the best-known novel by the late Beat writer William Burroughs. The book was a disjointed depiction of a heroin junky's life, full of wild hallucinatory images and graphic sex. It had been banned as pornography when it first came out in the 1950s. There was no *Naked Lunch 2*, so the screen-name suggested (at least to Kidd) that George and Mallory Flucker liked to take lunch in the nude. Two Neo Beats going to lunch naked and seeing things as they really are—naked and unadorned. Reality on a fork. Pretty witty, really.

Kidd smiled. But his smile faded when he reread the catchphrase: "Lost roads are our specialty." If the Fluckers truly knew about lost roads, then they might actually *be* fantastic investigators—or more accurately, investigators of the fantastic. Because the notion of lost roads was a fantastic one. More likely, they were crackpot psychics or New Age charlatans. But still…

"Give 'em a call," Rita said. "See what it's all about. But watch your back."

He nodded, then slipped the card into his shirt pocket. He downed the rest of his drink and then stood. "Put it on my tab," he said.

"That one's on the house," she said. "Welcome home, Kidd"

"Thanks, Rita."

She lit a cigarette. "Your bunk's just the way you left it. Manuel fixed your leaky faucet and sprayed for roaches. I didn't need to remind him how you hate having your stuff messed with."

Kidd looked at her with a warmth of feeling that surprised him. His former shrink would've said Rita was most certainly the classic mother surrogate, but Kidd didn't think so. Though she was nearly as old as his mother had been when she died six years ago in the wreckage of the family car, Rita didn't fit the mother mold. Unless your mother was a heavily tattooed fortyish former biker with a nostalgic fondness for barroom brawls and hell-raising for the joyous hell of it. Rita had mellowed since her youthful rowdy days, but if you scratched her hard-shell surface, you would quickly find her old outlaw-biker colors under there like a second skin, and then if you were smart you'd back off before she went nuclear on your ass.

"Appreciate it," he said, reaching down to pick up his bulky back-pack. "Where is ol' Manuel?"

"Ah, he's puttering around with the hog, trying to get it running again," she said, broodingly referring to her vintage Harley-Davidson that she hadn't ridden at all in the three years Kidd had known her. "I told him I didn't want it running. Too much of a temptation, you know? I'd be liable to saddle up and ride off into the sunset, never to be seen again. And I've got too much invested in the Hoot'n'Holler to do that. But you know I would. Dammit."

Kidd grinned at her. "Some day I'd like to see you in the saddle," he said. "See you just the way God made you."

"See this?" she said, waving the bar rag as if swatting away a fly. "What you see is what I am."

"I see," he said, taking his Nikon from a zippered compartment of the backpack. "I see more than you think. Just ask the Fluckers."

He removed the lens cover, brought the Nikon to his eye, pulled her image into focus and clicked a rapid series of shots.

"You'd be surprised what I think," she said, one-upping him. Ignoring the Nikon, she let the cigarette dangle from her lips as she took a small stack of glass ashtrays out from under the bar and dealt them like clunky cards along its length. "Even with that spooky brainiac thing you got going on."

Kidd shrugged. He put the camera away, put on his ballcap and shouldered his backpack. Any overt reference to his powers of intellect made him uneasy, though he couldn't have said why.

High IQ and a low tolerance for reality, as one psychologist had put it, and the words of that unofficial diagnosis had stuck with him like a psychic tattoo and haunted him whenever they came to mind.

"Don't you want something to eat?" she asked. "I'll throw a burger on the griddle."

"Maybe later. I wanna hit the shower and wash off some road grime."

"Let me know what you find out from the Fluckers," she said, her lips twisting up into a near-smile around her cigarette when she said the couple's name. Then she leaned over the bar and said, "But take care you don't get Flucked."

* * *

Kidd lived in a small cinderblock building behind Rita's roadhouse in Hoot Owl Hollow. It wasn't home so much as it was homebase, a place to which he regularly (but not *too* regularly) returned for short intervals between his road-ranging expeditions. It was a repository for the information he gathered on the road, a scavenger's stony den with a desk, a chair, a bed, a laptop computer and a metal filing cabinet stuffed with his photos, maps, drawings and road-trip effluvia.

He didn't have an actual home. He didn't want one. There was danger in staying too long or too often in one place. It was prudent to stay on the move.

The last thing he wanted was a troc tracking him back to this cinderblock lair.

He dug his rabbit's-foot keychain out of his jeans pocket, stuck the key in the lock and turned it. The tumbler snapped the bolt back and the door swung open. He stepped inside, knowing something was wrong. The air was too fresh. Outside had found its way inside.

He flipped the wall switch. The light came on and he saw that the place had been tossed. The filing cabinet drawer hung open and file folders were scattered about the floor, as were many of his photos and drawings.

The window in the rear wall was up, the pane broken out, indicating that the intruder had slipped in through the window. Was this a random break-in, the work of some petty burglar looking for money or valuables? No, because the MacBook was still here. And the intruder had left it open.

Someone had come looking for information. Someone who wanted to know what Kidd knew.

The follicles on the back of his neck prickled against his collar. A chill slithered up his spine.

CHAPTER TWO

Kidd left his ransacked living quarters and walked the twenty yards to Manuel's garage.

It was a double-bay cinderblock structure not much bigger than Kidd's abode, dwarfed by the roadhouse, yet lending the roadside oasis a grease monkey's mystique that Rita relished. She'd had the garage built for her old amigo and shade tree mechanic Manuel Cervantes and had been very happy to set him up in business. He was her wizard with a wrench. All she wanted in return was the special ambience of having a working garage on her property and ten percent of the profits, if there were any. Rita was proud of her biker past and didn't mind her customers knowing that she had ridden many a road with her legs forked over a snarling motorcycle. Her reputation alone was enough to keep some of the rowdier customers from getting too far out of line, and when the laying-on of hands *was* required, the former biker babe could hold her own in bum-rushing a burly drunk out the door and into the sobering mountain air. And you'd best not call her *biker babe* to her face.

Manuel stood by Rita's prized Harley, wiping his hands on a grease-blackened faded red rag. He was a wiry man of medium height, in his early fifties. His Zapata mustache, dark eyes and hooked nose gave him the look of a bandito of the late 1800's, but Manuel was as honest as a devout priest and wouldn't have been caught dead (or alive) carrying a *pistola*.

"Keed," he said when he looked up at Kidd. Manuel spoke perfectly good English with barely a trace of an accent, but for reasons known only to himself, he always addressed Kidd as *Keed*. "You're back. Cool."

"Good to see ya," Kidd said.

They shook hands, then hugged with enough vigorous back-slapping to confirm their manliness.

When they disengaged, Kidd said, "Got a minute? I wanna show you something."

"Sure, I got minutes to burn." Manuel grinned. His moustache caterpillered. "If you got the fire."

Having a conversation with Manuel Cervantes was often akin to conversing with a Zen poet; his words led you into a maze of meanings and dared you to find your way to the heart of what he was really saying. More often than not, there would be an odd sort of truth waiting at the end of the right path. But sometimes you just got the odd. Worst case, you got devastated by the metaphorical Minotaur.

They walked across the autumn-stunted grass to Kidd's cinderblock pillbox. The evening air was growing crisper and cooler as twilight dimmed the hollow.

"Rita said you sprayed for bugs and fixed the faucet," Kidd said. "When was that?"

"Day before yesterday, why? Did I break something?"

"No, I'm sure you didn't." Kidd opened the door and waved Manuel inside. "But somebody did."

"Whoa," he said when he saw the way the place had been trashed. "Who would do this?"

"No clue," Kidd said.

"Somebody looking for *some*thing, man."

"Yeah, so it would seem."

"What kinda loot you stash here? Gold? Diamonds? Treasure map?"

"Maps, but not to treasure," Kidd said.

"I'll fix that window, no problem." Manuel looked around for more damage. Didn't see any. "This pisses me off. Anything missing?"

"Some drawings and a couple of maps, I think."

"Drawings of what?"

Kidd tried to appear nonchalant. "Nothing valuable. Just some… drawings of my mythical creatures."

Manuel shot him a bemused expression. "No offense, Keed, but nobody in his right mind would steal those things."

"So, we're looking for somebody in his wrong mind. That may not be far from the truth."

"Uh-huh," Manuel said with mock wariness. "Why you draw those creepy things anyway?"

Kidd shrugged. "Sort of a hobby."

"A hobby. Yeah. Maybe you should switch to stamp collecting. Model trains. Something, hombre. Something that won't attract the weirdos."

"What I can't figure out is how they...he knew about me. About my drawings."

"Maybe he didn't. Maybe it was just some punk-ass kid looking to score, sees those far-out monsters you draw...or maybe you're right, he does know you and knew what he was looking for."

Kidd nodded.

"What about the missing maps? Maps to what?"

Kidd was tempted to come clean with Manuel and tell him the whole truth, tell him he'd spent the last three years trying to track trocs and to discover where and how they slipped into and out of this world. But he knew he couldn't do that without sounding like a full-blown paranoiac with dangerous delusions, so he said, "Places I've been. I like to keep a record of my travels. Just another of my eccentric hobbies."

Manuel smiled. "Someday you will stop bullshitting me and tell me the truth." He tapped his chest. "Manuel knows. He knows you're not just this weird guy with strange hobbies and wandering feet. You love the road but you won't drive a vehicle. You're the only guy I know who's made a career of hitchhiking, but it's a career that don't pay, so it ain't really a career. You're a man of contradictions, Keed. You don't add up. You don't even subtract down. And I don't even wanna think about you multiplying."

"Hey..."

"That last part was humor. Be fruitful and multiply, I don't care." His Zapata fringed a grin. "I think maybe you were born into the wrong era. Look at you. Bill Hickok-looking dude in North Georgia hillbilly country, no badge, no gun. No town to clean up. Out of place and out of your time. Just flipping lost."

"If I told you the real story, you wouldn't believe it. And you'd probably write me off."

"I'm hurt you should even think that. Manuel never writes off his friends."

"Sorry." Kid shrugged. "But you don't know how crazy the truth would sound."

"Try me."

"Maybe someday. When the time is right."

"Time ain't right or wrong. Time ain't nothing but the ticking."

"Yeah, but timing is everything, most of the time."

"Now you sound like me." Manuel grinned again. "Talking in riddles. That's what Rita says anyway."

Kidd began picking up the spilled papers and tucking them back into the file-folders. He was sorely tempted to unburden himself to Manuel. Tell him everything and let the chips fall. Manuel was an honorable man, the most honorable man Kidd knew. If he said he wouldn't write him off, then he wouldn't. But would he think less of Kidd for harboring such "crazy" beliefs? Toss-up.

Manuel was a voracious reader, a connoisseur of that brand of fiction known as magical realism. His particular favorites were those South American writers who apparently pioneered the genre of realistic fantasy. So...Manny might not find Kidd's story so hard to swallow. He might even enjoy it. But would he believe it? No. Nobody in his right mind would believe it without hard proof. So what would be the point in telling him? *To relieve psychic pressure. To make yourself feel better, at least temporarily.*

"You really want to hear my story?" Kidd asked as he stacked the files on his desk. "Let's get a pitcher of beer, hunker down in a corner booth, and I'll tell you the truth as I know it."

Manuel smiled. "Now you're talking."

On the way out, Kidd saw the small crystal of rose quartz on his pillow and he knew without doubt the identity of his intruder.

*   *   *

He shook his head and smiled as his memory conjured a vivid snapshot of Rose Rivers in khaki shorts, white T-shirt and hiking boots, a rock hammer in her hand. She is mining a roadcut for worthless treasure. The summer sun has turned her thin limbs the color of weak tea. Her light-brown hair is chopped short and the bill of a dirty beige ballcap shades her face. Rosie the rock hound. Kidd's blood sister.

He looked at the small scar on the pad of his left thumb and remembered how solemn she had been during the blood-letting ceremony. He hadn't wanted to cut himself but did it anyway because he knew she needed someone to trust, and true trust, according to Rose, had to be born in blood. He picked up the piece of quartz. Rose's calling card.

"What?" Manuel gave him a quizzical look.

"I know who did it. This girl I know."

"You must've pissed her off pretty good, Romeo." Manuel nodded toward the broken window.

"It's not like that. We're just friends. Bughouse alumni."

"Looks like she might need her medication adjusted."

Kidd shrugged. "How about a rain-check on that pitcher of beer?"

"Whatever you say, Keed. Tape some cardboard over that window and I'll fix it first thing in the morning."

"Right. Thanks, man."

Manuel headed back to his garage, and Kidd straightened up his living quarters, wondering what had prompted Rose to break in. She always used prepaid disposable cell phones with different numbers, so he couldn't call her to ask. He would have to wait for her to come to him. She was one of the few people he'd ever told about the trocs. He had even told her that he believed his close encounter with the creature at the scene of the deadly accident had somehow cured him of his mental illness. "The old scratch and lick," Rose had said, knowingly. "The thing's saliva got in your bloodstream and inoculated you. Wish I could meet up with one of those bad boys."

"But why didn't it kill me too?" he'd asked, more or less rhetorically.

"Because you were just a pipsqueak? Who knows, dude? Maybe it didn't like the way you smelled. The thing is, it gave you a gift, whether it meant to or not. So now you can see them when nobody else can."

"But I saw that first one before it ever touched me."

"Because of your bugged-out mental condition. Probably surprised the shit out of the lizardy son of a bitch, too."

During his psychiatric hospitalizations, Kidd had acquired firsthand knowledge of a variety of mental conditions and had come to believe that mental handicaps often came with unusual gifts of perception or with uniquely original thought processes. Some patients who saw things that weren't there were actually getting glimpses of other realities, of things that were there but were invisible to the "normies."

Rose was a prime example. Her documented diagnosis was Undifferentiated Schizophrenia with bipolar features. Though she wasn't overtly paranoid, she'd cobbled a complex delusional system at the center of her reality and lived her life accordingly. She was a geology major at the University of Georgia when she had her first psychotic break, and ever since, she believed her mission in life was to chip away at Mother Earth's skin until she discovered the deepest secrets of planetary existence. Every rock and mineral she collected was a key piece to the geological puzzle that would eventually lead her to a face-to-face meeting with the elusive Earth Goddess.

He had met her in a private psychiatric hospital north of Atlanta and they'd fallen into an easy friendship. Not long after their release, he'd tagged along on a weeklong rock-hunting expedition, and the experience had taught him that her passion for the planet was her religion and that she was a dedicated seeker of stony truth. Her single-minded reverence for Mother Earth was no odder than a devout Christian's love for Jesus Christ. Her devotion to the planet was apolitical, which Kidd found refreshing. If her obsession for finding sacred stones was delusional, it was harmless. She was in constant communion with the earth and it made her happy. Thanks to Rose, Kidd had acquired an appreciation of deep geological time—which gave him a new perspective on the trocs' phenomenal intrusions. He'd shared it with her by the campfire, using her as sounding board for his unfinished theory.

"Suppose they come here from the depths of time. Past or future, but probably past because they look prehistoric, you know? They're not extraterrestrial. The ones I've seen obey the same laws of gravity we do, with frightening agility. They're definitely of the earth. But I think they may be of a different time or maybe from an alternate earthly reality or dimension with its own deep time. You see what I'm getting at? That would explain the way they come out of nowhere to haunt the roads like ghostly beings, invisible to the average person."

Rose had been receptive to his theory, even though the focus of her obsessive pursuits was very much grounded on *terra firma*. "Invisible to everybody but you. Because you're a chosen one. Yeah, I get it."

"You think I'm nuts."

"Nuts make the man." A big Rosie grin.

"I'm serious."

"I know, Kidd-o. You wouldn't be you if you weren't. I'm just saying you're gonna need a big pair of *cojones* to take on your trocs. They sound like real bad dudes. You've been chosen for a reason, right? That's all I'm saying."

"You think I see myself as some sort of avenger, don't you?"

"No, dude, I don't pretend to know why Gaia put you on this path. That's for you to figure out."

Gaia was the broad-breasted Greek goddess personifying the earth, the revered deity to which Rose paid fealty.

"Because I'm not an avenger. I'm just trying to understand how they infiltrate and why. Not that I wouldn't love to nail one for dissection."

"Would it be murder if you did? Could you kill one in cold blood?"

"Like the one that killed my father?"

"But maybe he was already dying. From his injuries. How do you know they aren't moral creatures?"

"Because they *cause* accidents. So they can feed on death. The roads are where they feed."

Rose laughed. "If our shrinks could hear us now, they'd sign papers on us. Couple of bughouse refugees shooting the crazy-ass psycho shit. Living the dream, dude."

Kidd came back from his reverie and put the rose quartz in his pocket. He taped a piece of cardboard over the broken windowpane and then took a shower. He wrapped a towel around his waist and used his cell phone to call the Fluckers.

CHAPTER THREE

"This is George Flucker."

"You left your card at the Hoot'n'Holler. What do you want with me?"

"Is this William Kidd?"

"Yes."

"*The* William Kidd?" Flucker's voice betrayed his excitement.

"Yeah?"

"Thanks for calling, William. Damned good of you, considering you don't know me from Adam."

"Nobody calls me William. Kidd will do."

"Okay, Kidd. Believe me, I understand about names, as you can imagine, with the one I was born to."

"Who told you about me?" Kidd was fairly certain he already knew the answer.

"That cute little firecracker, Rose. Miss Rivers. The wife and I ran into her on the road." Flucker chuckled. "We didn't literally run into her. We met her in a roadside eatery and we struck up a conversation. Mallory and I told her of our singular vocation and the conversation led to you, in a roundabout way. It was all innocent enough, I assure you."

"And your vocation is 'fantastic investigator.'" Kidd laced his comment with cynicism.

The man chuckled again. "That never fails to raise a few brows. Stimulates curiosity, you know. And curiosity is essential in our business."

"What exactly is your business, and what's your business with me?" Kidd used the same confrontational tone he usually used with garden-variety telemarketers—which was exactly what George Flucker sounded like.

"It would be better if we could talk in person. Moreover, Mallory and I would love to meet you."

"Your card mentioned 'lost roads.' What's that supposed to mean?"

"Surely you know. It has to do with your *trocs*, I think. Miss Rivers told us about your activities along those lines."

"Did she also tell you she has a serious mental condition?"

"As a matter of fact, she did. She said you two met in a mental hospital."

Kidd bit his lower lip to keep his anger in check. He was angry at Rose for betraying his confidence, and angry at Flucker for his pushy salesman-like intrusiveness. He said, "I don't like having my privacy invaded, Mr. Flucker. Whatever you're selling, I don't want any."

Kidd tapped his cell to end the call.

Flucker called back immediately. Kidd let it ring, fuming. After the sixth ring, he answered with silence.

"Kidd, please," said Flucker, "this is very serious. We're not selling anything. We just need your…special talent. Let Mallory and I buy you dinner and just listen to what we have to say. Then if you still don't want anything to do with us, we'll thank you for your time and go away, never to bother you again."

Kidd said nothing.

George Flucker lowered his voice and said, "We found one. We actually rode a *stolen road*. Kidd, it was fantastic! No other word for it."

"Where are you now?" Kidd asked.

"Dahlonega. Are you at the roadhouse?"

"Yeah. Come now. I'll hold a booth."

"Great. We'll be there in about an hour. You won't regret this, I promise you."

Kidd broke the connection. He didn't like promises. Like lost and defenseless children, promises were fragile things in a sharp-edged world.

*   *   *

Rita was right. George Flucker looked like a rundown priest. His ruddy complexion suggested a lifelong weakness for the grape, and his eyes, slightly sunken above beefy cheeks, were eyes that had seen much sin and suffering, sad eyes that promised no remedy for the miseries you were sure to endure. He was pleasant enough on the surface, but no amount of gregariousness could hide his underlying world-weary melancholy.

Mallory Flucker was a different story, a self-styled refugee from a romance novel with a tragic ending, a displaced heroine with too much heart and a down-home soul—heart and soul a tad too ripe for the taking. She was a bosomy woman in her mid-forties who somehow managed to look natural in the cowboy hat she wore on her wiry bleached-blond hair. She looked like Dolly Parton without all the glitter and cosmetic glamour. Kidd figured she was her husband's lifeline, the loving mother figure that kept George from sinking into booze-soaked despair. She was just the sort of woman Rose would open up to without hesitation. And as a lapsed Catholic, Rose would've fallen into easy intimacy with Mallory's priest-like spouse. Little wonder that Rose had confessed too many secrets to these two.

Mallory didn't take her hat off as she settled into the booth across from Kidd. The Hoot'n'Holler was the kind of place where you left your hat on when you sat down to eat, and she appeared very much at home here. George slid in next to her and gave Kidd a sad smile.

"Miss Rivers was right," George said. "You do look a little like Bill Hickok."

"Watch out for those aces and eights," Mallory said, smiling tentatively.

"I never touch cards," Kidd said. "They're instruments of the devil."

Mallory's mouth dropped. "Really?"

"No, not really." Kidd allowed a smile on his lips. "But I don't like to play games."

George gave him a priestly Ah-yes-my-son nod and said, "Good to know."

"You got me," said Mallory, touching her breast. "Good feint. You got game, as the kids say. Do they still say that?"

Kidd said, "Touché." Mrs. Flucker was sharper than she looked. As was her doppelganger Dolly Parton, a shrewd businesswoman who was more than the sum of her outsized boobs and sugar-cured voice. "You caught me gaming you."

A deep recognition flashed in her eyes. "I'm just a simple country gal," she said, batting her mascara-lengthened lashes, "but I'm hard to hoodwink."

"I see that," said Kidd, relaxing a little.

George cleared his throat in phlegmy preamble, then said, "Order anything you like. Then we'll explain why we need you. That top sirloin is very good, but I guess you know that, since this is your homebase. According to Miss Rivers."

"She obviously told you a lot about me. And you want to believe it's all true."

"Given what we already know, it certainly has the ring of truth."

"What exactly do you know? You mentioned the roads."

Rita came over to the booth to take their order. She didn't often wait tables, preferring to leave that job to big-haired Kim, but she was curious about the Fluckers. "What'll you folks have tonight?"

She winked at Kidd, who rolled his eyes. The Fluckers ordered steak dinners and Kidd ordered a grilled bacon and cheese sandwich.

"We've spent three years studying lost roads," George said when Rita was out of earshot.

"Your specialty," Kidd said in reference to their business card, his tone skeptical.

"Well, we're hardly specialists on the subject, since so little is known, but it is the area of our special interest. We put that on the card as a hook, hoping to make contact with true fellow travelers. So to speak."

"I'll bet you get a lot of kooks on the hook. Coming out of the woodwork like alien abductees."

"We have investigated a number of alleged UFO abductions," Mallory said, "and ninety percent of them were obviously bogus. We're not New Age kooks or con artists, Kidd. We're very serious about what we do."

"And you found a lost road."

"We did indeed," George said.

"We were lucky we made it back," said Mallory.

"It was amazing," George went on. "It took us into a different world. A land so strange I'm at a loss to describe it."

"We were scared poopless." Mallory leaned forward and lowered her voice. "But we wanted to keep going to see where it would take us. Like something was pulling us deeper into that strange landscape."

"But then we saw those shadow things and we chickened out, turned around and came back."

"What shadow things?" Kidd asked.

George shrugged. "We couldn't really see *them*. We only saw their shadows. The things making the shadows were nothing but blurs of ghostly motion."

Mallory nodded enthusiastically. "Ghostly motion, that's the perfect way to put it."

"There were five or six of them running along the road ahead of us, as if leading us." George steepled his hands in front of his face. "It wasn't until Miss Rivers told us about your trocs that we put it all together and concluded that the things we almost saw probably were those same creatures."

"Tell us what they look like," Mallory said. "Rose said you said they were like lizardy insects."

"That's not what I said. *Lizardy* is not something I would've said."

"Describe them for us," George said. "We've learned not to trust secondhand reportage."

"It would be easier just to show you my drawings," Kidd told them. "But they do have the look of insectlike lizards. Six or seven feet tall. If a giant praying mantis mated with a giant lizard, you'd get something like a troc. And they are incredibly fast on their feet."

"Why do you call them that?" Mallory asked. "Trocs?"

"Their skin is like a crocodile's, though they're not thick-bodied like a croc. Troc just popped into my head. From the place of secret names, I guess. It seemed to fit."

"And that scar under your eye?" Mallory's face showed motherly concern.

"Just as Rose must've told you, that's where one clawed me and then licked my blood."

"Jeez," Mallory said with a shudder. "You must've been terrified."

Kidd shrugged. "I think I was in shock from the wreck and from seeing what the thing did to my father. Not to mention the fact that I was clinically psychotic at the time."

"Exactly what did it do to your father?" George asked.

"I can't say. I mean I don't really know, but my impression at the time was that it sucked the life out of him. Or the soul. Like the silly myth of a cat sucking a baby's breath and killing it. Dad would've died of his injuries anyway, but still…"

"And you believe it cured you of your…mental condition?" George asked.

"I do."

"And left you with the singular ability to see them whenever they venture into our world."

"I can't prove it, but that's what I believe. I think I was able to see that first one because of my biochemical imbalance."

"How many have you seen, all told?"

"Six. So far. Separate sightings."

After a long moment of thoughtful silence, George Flucker said, "You might be the only person in the world who wears the mark of a troc. In primitive cultures, that would make the beast your totem animal and that scar would be considered sacred."

"Your point being?"

"I'm not sure. I'm only trying to get a handle on it, put it in historic perspective. I don't know what the hell it means. But I'm intrigued by the possibility that the creature could be your totemic guardian. It let you live, after all. And it gave you a gift, of sorts."

"Or maybe it put its mark on me to let the others know it had claimed me for later. Maybe they don't do small fry."

"Catch and release," Mallory offered. "Throw the little ones back."

Kidd nodded. Then he said, "Tell me how you found the road."

"A tip from a trucker took us to it," George said. "He saw one of our cards at a truck-stop outside of Memphis and called us."

"He was an ex-Marine, Iraq War vet," Mallory said. "Not normally the kind of guy to give a second thought to urban legends like lost roads. No Post-traumatic Stress in this guy. Rock-solid."

"He was a very credible witness," said George. "Long story short, his tip took us to a stretch of Georgia road a hundred miles northwest of here. Naturally we went right away but all we found was an ordinary blacktop. He'd mentioned that he found the road under a full moon, so we waited for the next full moon and tried again. And by God, there it was. One minute we're cruising along a run-of-the-mill state road and the next we're riding a ghost road into another world with an escort of shadowy roadrunners."

"That or we were both having the same lunatic hallucination," said his wife.

"What was so otherworldly about it?" Kidd asked.

"You have to see it for yourself, Kidd." George grinned. "In three days the moon's full again. Ride along and we'll take you there and you can see the otherworld for yourself."

CHAPTER FOUR

Kidd scarcely tasted his sandwich. He ate on autopilot as he listened to the Fluckers go on about their upcoming expedition to an unknown land. He occasionally asked questions, but mostly he just listened to their excited talk and very quickly became caught up in their enthusiasm.

Since their short ride on the ghost road a month ago, they had been busy preparing for their next foray. This time they intended to do it properly, using available technology to record as much data as possible. They'd equipped their vehicle with a dashboard compass in case of an electrical failure. They had shelled out for a GPS, an expensive night-vision digital movie camera, camping gear, guns and ammo, a first-aid kit, and a month's supply of food and bottled water, the food mostly Trail-mix and canned fruit.

"Of course, we aren't planning on staying the whole month till the next full moon," George explained, "but we want to be prepared in the unlikely event we do get stuck there. Truth be told, we're not even sure it's possible to stay over there any length of time." Then he went on to voice his half-baked theory of the full moon's effect on invisible earth tides, which somehow opens the passage to the ghost road and allows access to the parallel world. "It's not much of a theory, I admit, but somehow the moon does have an effect on *some*thing. Gravity, electromagnetic waves, who knows? I'm not a physicist. And of course, I'm using 'parallel world' metaphorically, not geometrically or the way quantum physicists use it."

By the end of the meal, Kidd had learned that George and Mallory had attempted to find the same mystery road for a return trip two days after their first venture. "It took us that long to get our courage up for a second try," Mallory said. But the second attempt failed, so they reasoned that they could only find it again on the night of the full moon. "A very narrow window of opportunity," George added. "Maybe just a matter of hours."

"How long do you intend to stay over there?" asked Kidd. "If you do manage to get back there."

"We figure two or three hours should be safe," George answered. "We'll stay close to the point of egress. Lord knows, we don't want to get lost and lose the way back home. We'll park the vehicle there and proceed on foot just a short distance, keeping the vehicle in sight."

"And take your chances with the trocs," said Kidd.

"That's where you come in. You can see the buggers and if they show signs of aggression, you'll have to shoot them in self-defense. We're not going in as big-game hunters but if we happen to bag one and take it back with us, imagine the splash that would make in the scientific community."

"So basically, you want me to ride shotgun on your expedition."

"Well, yes, that's part of it." George looked a little embarrassed.

"What do you say?" Mallory asked, smiling. "Are you…game?"

"Of course he is," said George. "We've found what he's been look-ing for most of his adult life. Right, Kidd?"

"If all this is true, then yes, I would have to be in. But it's hard to believe. No offense, but for all I know, you're a just couple of fruitcakes."

"You know we're not," Mallory said in a scolding tone. "You, of all people, know better than that."

Kidd looked at her, then looked at her cleric-like husband. He nod-ded. "Pencil me in. I'll give you a definite answer tomorrow."

"Good enough," George said with a slightly sagging smile. "You know how to handle a rifle?"

*   *   *

Sitting in the quiet of his bunker-like living quarters, Kidd studied the contents of the file folder the Fluckers had given him. George and Mallory had gone to check into a nearby motel, taking with them several drawings Kidd had made of the trocs he'd seen. The painstaking detail of the drawings had clearly given them pause. The creatures looked dangerous, hideously menacing. That was good, Kidd thought. They needed a healthy dose of fear. Taking on trocs was serious business, not fun-and-games.

As he perused the pages in the folder, he realized that the Fluckers had indeed been very serious about their research on "lost roads." Through the Internet and through face-to-face interviews with a handful of individuals claiming to have seen strange stretches of roads, the Fluckers had systematically mapped the locations of "legitimate" sightings and had written up their findings with a minimum of speculative conclusions. Two sightings in Tennessee, one in Pennsylvania, two in Kansas, one in Colorado, and three in Georgia.

Included in the packet was "A Brief History of Stolen Roads" by George and Mallory Flucker, which apparently had been printed out from their website. According to the authors, the first known incident occurred in 1945, on a country road outside of Birmingham, Alabama. A long-haul trucker reported that he'd gotten lost one night on a "spooky" stretch of blacktop and suddenly found himself in a landscape that looked like "something from another planet." There were no road signs, and no dividing lines painted on the road. The road itself looked ancient and the trucker said he got the feeling that it wasn't a manmade road at all but something the earth might've "grown." "When I smelled ozone and the hairs on my arms stood up like lightning was about to strike, I turned around and got the heck out of there, back the way I came."

In 1966 a middle-aged widow on her way to visit relatives got lost on her familiar route from her home in Philadelphia to a small town in southern Pennsylvania and ended up "on an unearthly road in the middle of nowhere." A large animal "the likes of which I ain't never seen before" caused her to run off the road. She turned around and sped back the way she'd come until she found familiar landmarks. Her son-in-law, who happened to be the editor of a small-town weekly newspaper, wrote up a tongue-in-cheek story of her sighting. The article quoted her: "It was like I was riding on a stolen road, like somebody'd

just *shanghaied* the road and plopped it down in some foreign land."
Thus, *stolen roads* entered the esoteric lexicon of popular culture.

In 1999 a military policeman on active-duty leave from Fort Benning, Georgia, was riding a back-road shortcut to I-75 when the "road suddenly began to hum" under the wheels of his sports car. The eerie humming sound grew so loud that he cut his speed, thinking that something might be wrong with the vehicle. The noise became so shrill that he stopped on the side of the road and turned off the motor, but the humming continued, rising in pitch "like a pressure-cooker getting ready to blow the lid off." Then he noticed the road ahead in his headlights seemed to be wavering "like it was turning to dark liquid." Under the light of the full moon, the land on both sides of the road looked raw and broken, as if it had just erupted from below the surface in an earthquake. He turned around and backtracked until the painful noise ceased and he was back on familiar land. He immediately reported the incident to the Georgia State Patrol, and then proceeded to his Atlanta destination. When he called back the next day, a State Trooper told him that the unit dispatched to the location had found nothing but ordinary road and no sign of disturbed ground. The trooper had advised him to "Lay off the hooch when you're behind the wheel."

On October 29, 2008, the wife of a prominent fundamentalist minister in Jasper, Georgia, had a flat tire and stopped on the side of a mountain road. She used her cell phone to call her husband because she didn't know how to change the SUV's tire. Night was falling and she turned on her hazard flashers. She declined the assistance of a passing motorist, preferring to wait for her husband. She was wary of strangers, especially at night, on a lonely road. All at once she felt lightheaded and fearful, though she didn't know why she should feel that way. Her ears began to ring as the air pressure abruptly changed. She turned the headlights on bright. The road in front of her looked "like a black ribbon floating in the air." She shut her eyes and began to pray "for deliverance from something awful, though I didn't know what." When she opened her eyes, the landscape before her had become hellish. "I thought it must be the Rapture and that I was being left behind in some kind of hell on earth." In panic, she started the car, turned around and rode away on the flat. "I never drove that road again," she said later. When her husband asked her to describe the hellish landscape, she refused, stating that she couldn't talk about it because it was "too real."

Kidd's cell phone chirped. He answered.

"Kidd-o? That you?"

"No, it's the Easter bunny."

"Oh, cool. Lay me a pretty egg, Brother Long Ears"

"Rose, you know why I'm pissed at you, right?"

"I'm not Rose anymore. I changed my name to Rocky."

"Of course you did."

"Rocky Rivers. Dig it, big daddy."

"Why did you tell those people about my personal business?"

"Which people?"

"Shit. Who did you tell besides the Fluckers?"

"Nobody. Unless you count this hitchhiker dude I met in the Rockies. And he didn't believe it anyway. Thought I was nuts, but he was the one with serial killer eyes."

"You are nuts."

"Oh, and you're Mister Normal now? Give me a break. I thought you'd be pissed about the window."

"I *am* pissed about the window. Why'd you break in?"

"I got scared."

"Of what?"

"Trocs and things. You know. The Big Nowhere."

"So you broke in, wrecked my place and stole some of my stuff."

"Seemed like a good idea at the time. I needed some of your juju. Whaddya want? Me to kiss your ass and say I'm sorry?"

"Where are you?"

"Closer than you think. Drop your drawers, Wild Bill, and I'll apologize."

"Where are you?" he asked again.

"I'm tooling along in my Toyota pagoda, looking for Nirvana or a place to crash. Move over, rover, let Rocky come over."

"How long have you been off your meds?"

"Not long enough. Rocky don't need no steeking meds. And no steeking batches either."

"You can sleep on the floor but I'm not up for an all-night bullshit session."

"Land ho! I'm docking at the Hoot even as we speak. You in your crib?"

"Yeah."

"I'll grab some beers from Rita and be there in two shakes of a lamb's dick. Rocky Rivers out."

Ten minutes later Rose was at Kidd's door, a bottle of beer in each hand. She gave one to him and said, "Peace offering, White Eyes." Then she leaned into him and whispered: "Don't freak out but I think I've got a troc on my tail."

CHAPTER FIVE

He pulled her inside and shut the door against the night. "What do you mean, you've got a troc on your tail?"

She took a pull from her bottle, belched, and then said, "I shit you not, I saw one. Just now, on the road."

"Bullshit."

"You think you're the only one who can see them? Uh-uh, I saw the ugly fucker. It was hanging off the back of this eighteen-wheeler, giving me the finger."

"Yeah, right."

"I did. It was."

"You've got rocks in your head." He suppressed a smile.

She gave him a big grin and then planted a kiss on his lips. "Drop your britches and I'll kiss your ass too."

"No thanks." He took a sip of beer.

Rose pulled a pack of cigarettes from the pocket of her baggy cargo shorts and fired one up with the Zippo her recently deceased father had scored long ago in Vietnam. "Want one?"

He shook his head.

"They won't kill you, you know. They only kill people with long lives, and you and me are short-timers on this earth, for sure."

"So you keep telling me."

"True. Only the good die young. Like the song says. It's all there in the lyrics of all those smarmy pop songs, the secret soul of America laid bare in dipshit clichés and bad poetry."

"Not much of a secret then."

"Not if you know how to read the hidden meanings. But you can't do it without the key. Stevie Wonder nearly gave away the whole shooting match with his 'Songs in the Key of Life.' But what the hell, he's blind so we'll have to cut him some slack."

She sang the chorus of Stevie's "Higher Ground."

Her nipples poked out against her cotton T-shirt. She was small-breasted and never wore a bra. Though he thought of her as a kid sister, he sometimes felt a pang of sexual energy in her presence, an incestuous spark of dark electricity arcing between them. He blushed and looked away. He took another swig of beer.

"You staring at my tits again?" She gave him a lascivious smile. She sat cross-legged on his bed and snugged the bottle between her thighs.

"No. Not intentionally. They're hard to ignore, that's all."

"These little ol' things?" Cigarette dangling from her lips, she cupped her hands over her breasts.

He rolled his eyes.

She said, "You ought to just fuck me and get it over with."

"Rose!" he said, barking more than he meant to.

"Rocky, dammit. Rose doesn't live here anymore."

"Well, I'm sure not going to fuck somebody named Rocky."

"Well shit. A girl can't win with you, can she?"

"There's no winning to it."

"My point exactly." She tweaked her nipples. "Or should I say *points*." He scowled at her.

"You know I just like giving you a hard time," she said.

"Just cut it out, okay?"

"You're no fun. You need to lighten up, dude."

He sat at his desk and sipped his beer. "You didn't really see a troc."

She shrugged. "I thought I did. I saw something. Maybe my imagination filled in the details, thanks to your damn drawings. But it creeped me out, whatever it was." She inhaled deeply, then leaned forward, squinting in the smoke, and said, "Tell the truth. Are you gay?"

He chuckled. "Would it make any difference if I was?"

"No, and you know why? Because I'd still get into your jeans someday. It's destiny."

Kidd shook his head. "I'm not gay."

"Are you still a virgin?"

"What's with this preoccupation with sex?"

"Are you?"

"No."

"I get these intense cravings sometimes," she said. "Maybe it's from fondling rocks all the time. I'm like a bitch in heat and all I can think about is getting my rocks off."

"There's a calcified cliché. I think you spend too much time by yourself. Rocks aren't very sociable."

"Neither are you."

"Hey."

"Making me sleep on the floor? A gentleman would share his bed."

"You can have the bed," he said with a sigh. "I'll take the floor."

She grinned, then sucked on her cigarette as Kidd realized she'd shrewdly suckered him out of his bed for the night. She finished her beer and dropped the smoking butt in the bottle. The ember winked out with a wet hiss.

"So you met George and Mallory." she said.

"I did."

"Well?"

"They claim they've found a 'stolen road' and they want me to ride shotgun on their return trip."

"You gonna do it?"

"You know I am. How could I not?"

"Cool. I am too."

"I didn't know they invited you."

"They didn't. I'm inviting myself. If it's for real, then we should bring back rock samples, and I'm the perfect rockhound for the job."

"I don't think that's a good idea."

"Why not?"

"Too many unknowns. Too much that could go wrong."

"Oh, I get it. You think you have to protect me, keep me out of danger. Get over yourself, White Eyes. I can take care of myself. If I needed a keeper, I'd go back to the nuthouse."

"I just don't want anything to happen to you." He shrugged.

"There's probably nothing to worry about anyway. I doubt we'll find anything but an ordinary road. If these things always opened up in the same places, we'd already know they're for real, wouldn't we? It would be big news."

"Not if the government kept it secret."

"Please. A government conspiracy on top of an urban legend? Give me a break."

"For all you know, they could have trocs in captivity at some secret location. Like Area 51."

"Sure. And Elvis probably sings them lullabies to put them to sleep."

She laughed heartily. Then she broke into song, a ridiculous baritone rendition of "All Shook Up." Halfway through, she suddenly jumped up and announced that she wanted to sing in the shower.

"Knock yourself out," Kidd said.

She pulled off her shirt, dropped it on the floor and unsnapped her shorts.

He watched her undress, staring at her boyish nudity as she pranced into the bathroom and shut the door. Then the water was humming through the pipes and she was singing an ancient Dylan song about God and Abraham out on Highway 61.

*   *   *

At midnight they walked to the Hoot to share a pitcher of beer. The night had turned cold and Rose was wearing the too-big army fatigue jacket she'd inherited from her father and sun-faded worn-thin blue jeans. It was a weeknight and the roadhouse wasn't crowded. Rose ate fries covered in Ketchup, smoking a cigarette as she chewed. Kidd bummed a smoke. He coughed after the first inhalation, and didn't inhale much after that.

Rose said, "You need a smoking lesson. You smoke like a six-year-old."

"Six-year-olds smoke?"

"Hell yeah. You'd be surprised. Some of them chew too. Skoal is real popular with first-graders these days."

"When did you start hanging with grade-schoolers?"

"I keep my ear to the ground." She smiled enigmatically.

"Ah," he said, venting smoke through his nostrils. "Of course. Listening for the earth's whispered secrets."

"Mock me at your peril, Kidd-o. There may come a day when those secrets save your ass from a terrible fate."

"I'm not mocking you. I keep an open mind on this stuff."

She pointed a floppy French fry at him and said, "Then I'll let you in on one. Something big is in the wind. I've heard it rumbling up from the core of the earth. Like a tremor coming before a major quake."

"What, you're predicting earthquakes now?"

"No, not an earthquake, ninny. Another kind of quake. I don't know yet what it will be, but it will be big. Something that will change things at a fundamental level."

He didn't know what to say to that, so he said nothing.

"Maybe it will have something to do with the roads, your trocs and wherever they come from," she said, her expression uncharacteristically grim. "See, the earth has its own language and I'm not that good yet at translating it. But I'm getting there."

She pulled a small copper-colored rock from her pocket and set it on the table next to her plate of fries. "This is the holiest rock I've ever seen," she said. "I found it in Graves Mountain, Georgia. It's a mineral called rutile. Rutile is essentially titanium dioxide. Pretty, huh? It's a prophet gem, wise in the ways of Gaia. I sleep with it under my pillow so my subconscious can read bits of the dense message it carries in its crystal. It shapes my dreams sometimes. When the planet talks to me, it uses the language of dreams. This baby is *loaded* with knowledge. It's my dream stone. I know this sounds like loco bullshit but think of how much information can pass through a silicon chip. See what I'm saying? The earth is giant repository of stored information. If we ever learn how to plug into it the right way, we'll have direct access to the Goddess and her divine knowledge."

"That's deep. Way over my head, I'm afraid."

"No, man, it's not. It's elementary. It's the elements and their interactions with the planet and everything on it. Including us. The earth grew us, you know. Just as surely as it grows plants and trees. You're just not used to thinking about it this way. It's the universe in a grain of sand. And we're the big grains of fleshy sand and blood, bro. The balance of minerals in seawater is the same balance in the human body. We're stardust, dude. Like the song says. *Woodstock?* We are golden, bro. Once again, it's all there in the music."

Kidd pointed at the rock. "And that's like a crystal radio that broadcasts to your subconscious."

"Yeah, sort of like that. But I wouldn't exactly call it a receiver."

"And the earth grew the trocs. And whatever else we might find at the end of any stolen road."

"You got it. If there really is some other world out there, it's *of the earth*, no matter how unearthly it might seem. And it just might be Gaia's queendom. Which is why I'm going with you, so forget about trying to stop me or talk me out of it. I'm going, Kidd. Sure as the Goddess made little green apples and pretty pink nipples."

"It's not up to me. It's up to the Fluckers. This is their trip. I'm just along for the ride."

"Tell them you won't go unless I do. That ought to do the trick."

A commotion at the bar drew their attention. A big man with tattoos covering both arms was climbing over the bar, going after Rita. He hurled slurred curses as he topped the bar on hands and knees. Rita reached under the bar and came out with a baseball bat. Without hesitation, she whacked his hand with a sharp blow of the bat and the man howled and collapsed across the bar. Rita used the bat to push him back, and he sank to the floor, leaning against the barstool and hugging his broken hand to his chest.

"Leave now or I'll call the cops," Rita said, her voice steady and full of cold authority. "And don't ever show your ass in here again."

The man pulled himself up and shambled toward the door without looking back.

"Rita's full of the Goddess," Rose said with naked admiration. "Too bad *she's* not going with us."

CHAPTER SIX

Kidd woke to the sound of whispering. Eyelash-soft whispers sprinkled with mewling whimpers. He was on the floor, cocooned in his sleeping bag. He lifted his head and listened, trying to make out what Rose was saying in her sleep. Moonlight leaked in through the blinds and gave the dark room a ghostly glow. She floated on a bed of shadows, her body restless beneath bedcovers. The whispers grew louder but he couldn't decipher them.

He sat up and called her name softly. She didn't wake up, so he raised his voice: "Rose, wake up."

She came awake with a jerk of her legs. "Huh, wha…?"

"You were dreaming," he said.

"Whassat…?" She sat up.

"You were dreaming," he said again.

"Kidd? Where are you?"

"Down here."

"Don't *do* that. I thought you were the boogeyman."

"You were having a bad dream."

She held out her arms. "Come here."

He threw back the unzipped flap of the sleeping bag, got up and sat on the side of the bed. She pulled him to her in a clumsy hug. "Stay here," she whispered. "Keep me here. I don't wanna go back."

"Back where?" He lay down beside her. She was trembling as if cold, though her body was bed-warm.

"Wherever I was."

"You remember what you were dreaming?"

"Yeah, no, I dunno." Her voice was thick with sleep. "I'm not sure it *was* a dream."

"Okay. Go back to sleep. I'm here. It's okay."

A moment later she was asleep again, breathing softly in his ear. He thought she probably wouldn't remember in the morning how he'd come to lie beside her. He went to sleep wondering if her dream stone was under the pillow.

*   *   *

The rusted-out vehicles stand in the undergrowth of ropy vines like empty carapaces of ungainly beasts drawn here to die in desolation. Moonlight hazes window glass and chrome. Skeletons sit slumped behind the wheels of a few cars, but most are empty, their passengers long gone.

Kidd moves among the steel husks at a slow creep, taking care not to disturb the things lurking in viny darkness. Rose screams for help but he doesn't see her, cannot pinpoint her location. Her screams eat at him. He calls out to her, running now, desperate to find her before it's too late. Before those things rip her apart and feast on her innards. Leafy runners grab at his ankles as he lopes between a vine-covered SUV and an ancient pickup.

A motorcycle approaches, cutting a trail of moonlit dust across the wounded earth. Rita sits tall in the saddle as she roars up and shouts for him to get on behind her. "We have to get Rose," he yells, but Rita says, "It's too late. Get on."

From somewhere in the automotive graveyard come the sounds of fierce snarling and a terrible rending of flesh and snapping of bones. Rose's final scream reaches a wrenching crescendo and then abruptly ceases.

*   *   *

Kidd came awake with a violent start. Rose's soft breathing reassured him that she was safe. He slipped a hand under the pillow and found the cool stone, removed it and dropped it on the floor. He was a long time getting back to sleep, but when he finally did, he had no more nightmares. None that he remembered.

*   *   *

"Like trying to wake the dead."

Kidd opened his eyes. Rose was standing over him, grinning. Morning light filtered in through the blinds.

"Rise and shine, sleepyhead dead," she said.

"I don't feel like shining," he muttered.

"What was this doing on the floor?" She held her dream stone in front of his face.

"I had a nightmare." He sat up and put his feet on the floor.

"Tell," she said with too much enthusiasm so early in the morning.

"Coffee first. Then conversation."

"You'll forget details. Do it while it's still fresh." She shoved the stone in her jeans pocket.

"Trust me. I won't forget any of it."

"Must've been a humdinger, as my old granddaddy used to say." She giggled. "What is a humdinger, anyway? Sounds like some kind of sexual perversion to me, like a blow job with bells on."

Yawning, Kidd said, "*Hum* is a murmuring approval. *Dinger* a superlative thing. Early twentieth century origin, most likely."

"Where do you get this shit?"

He shrugged. "Word origin is sort of a hobby."

"You're pretty good at making them up too. Like *troc*. That's your best one yet."

"I doubt it'll ever make the dictionary."

"It might if we bring one back. Dead, of course. I'd hate to have to capture one, if they're as badass as you say."

"They are. And then some."

Kidd pulled on his jeans, threw on a shirt, and then went to the bathroom to relieve himself. When he came out, Rose was zipping up her backpack.

"You're not stealing anything else, are you?"

"I never stole anything. I just borrowed a couple of those drawings and a map. I was going to show them to George and Mallory but then you came back and now I don't have to."

"Breaking and entering is not cool."

"Toldja, I got scared. Cut me some slack."

"I have." He dropped his keys in his pocket. "Let's get that coffee."

"I've been thinking…"

"Uh-oh."

She socked his arm. "That maybe we *should* ask Rita to go with us."

Kidd remembered Rita riding up on her Harley in the dream. "Bad idea. She doesn't know anything about all this weird stuff and even if we told her she wouldn't believe a word. She certainly wouldn't go off on some wild-ass trip with a bunch of sideways New Age crazies and assorted crackpots. That's not her style."

"I guess you're right." She frowned. "But still, I'd feel better if she was going."

"You don't have to go, you know. If you're going to wig out, it would be better for everybody if you didn't."

"I won't wig out." She held out her scarred thumb. "Blood sister swear."

He touched his scarred thumb to hers. Then they interlaced their fingers and shook on it. Kidd tried not to think about the way she'd been screaming in his dream.

CHAPTER SEVEN

They got in Rose's mud-caked Toyota pickup and rode a quarter mile down the road to the Waffle House for breakfast. It was located just off the Interstate and was relatively crowded, so they had to wait ten minutes for a free booth. During the wait Rose was quieter than usual, and it wasn't until they were seated that she said, "We probably look like a couple of ex-mental patients to these people."

Kidd said, "Nah. We look more like a couple of homeless hippies lost in a time warp. Anyway, since when are you so sensitive about your past?"

"I don't know. Sometimes I feel like I'm on extended leave from the bughouse, like it's my true home." She softly sang a line from an old Simon and Garfunkel song: "I am a rock…I am an island."

"'Homeward Bound,'" he said, feeling a pang of sadness for her. She had alienated her family by pursuing a lifestyle they didn't condone, and she apparently had no intention of patching things up.

"But I'm not homeless. The road is my home. The earth protects me. The crazy house was never a home. You know how it is. It's the same for you."

"I've got the family mansion in Atlanta but I almost never go there. I don't believe in ghosts but every time I set foot in it, I feel my parents' presence. I'll probably sell it some day. But I'm doing all right on the trust fund."

The waitress came over to take their order. Rose ordered a stack of pancakes with bacon, and he ordered two eggs over easy with a side of sausage.

Rose took a sip of steaming coffee and said, "Wonder what they'd do if I lit up a smoke."

"Tell you to put it out."

"What if I refused?"

"They'd call the smoke patrol and you'd get a big fine."

"I don't like the way the world is going. Like it made a serious wrong turn a few years back and now it's on the road to post-hipster millennial hell, no turning back."

"Whaddya gonna do?" he said in poor imitation of a generic standup comedian. "If they don't get you coming, they get you going. No matter what you do, you're gonna get got."

"Amen, brother. Get it up the ass even when you don't want it."

They ate in comfortable silence. After a while she said, "You were gonna tell me about your dream."

"It was nothing. Not worth telling."

"Bullshit, White Eyes. Tell it." Calling him White Eyes was her way of reminding him that she had noble Cherokee blood in her background, on her mother's side.

Reluctantly, he described his dream, leaving nothing out.

She shuddered. "That gave me goose bumps, dude. Dying in the Big Nowhere. That'd be the big suck, being a midnight snack for trocs."

"I don't know if they were trocs. I couldn't see them."

"Wish you hadn't told me that shit."

"You asked."

"Yeah, but if it came from the stone, it could really happen that way."

"Like I said, you don't have to go with us."

She downed the last of her coffee with a faraway look in her eyes. "Fuck that. I'm going. Call 'em right now and tell 'em we're a package deal. Both of us or none of us. Take it or leave it."

Kidd pulled out his cell. "Here goes nothing," he said.

"No, bro. Here goes everything."

*　　*　　*

When George Flucker answered, Kidd said, "I'm in. With one stipulation. Rose Rivers goes too."

After a long pause, George said, "All right. Fine. So long as you think she can be counted on. A geologist would be an asset. Let's meet later today and we'll brief you on the plan. We should do a few practice runs so when it's time for the real thing, everybody knows his job. We want to make the most of our time over there."

"When and where?"

"We'll pick you up at the Hoot'n'Holler, say, at two this afternoon."

"Okay. We'll be here."

"Outstanding. Welcome aboard, Kidd. You won't regret it."

"I hope not." Kidd ended the call, then smiled at Rose and said, "Congratulations. You made the team."

"Bitchin'," she said with a wide grin.

*   *   *

Later in the day Rita cornered Kidd in the Hoot and asked him about the Fluckers. Rose was coming back from the ladies' room, ballcap sitting sidewise on her head, looking more boyish than usual.

"They wanted to talk to me about lost roads," he said. "You've heard of them, right? Lost roads, stolen roads, ghost roads?"

"I heard a couple of customers talking about that a while back. *National Enquirer* stuff, right?"

"Yeah, something like that."

"What are you, some kind of expert on the subject?"

"No, not really. Rose told them tales out of school about me, gave them the wrong impression."

Rose climbed onto the barstool next to him. "I hear my name mentioned?" she asked.

"I was telling Rita about the Fluckers," he said, hoping Rose could keep her mouth shut for once.

"Good people," said Rose. "My kind of peeps. Waay down to earth. I had to hook 'em up with Kidd-o for the wild ride."

Kidd cringed. He looked down at the bar and tried to maintain a poker face. He felt Rita's eyes on him.

"What aren't you telling me?" she asked. "I know there's more to it, so don't try and bullshit me."

"Tell her," Rose said. "She's cool."

Kidd said, "She already thinks I'm a couple of beers short of a sixpack."

"That's not true," Rita said, "and you know it. You don't wanna tell me? Fine. But don't make me out to be some square Jane who's too unhip to get it. I took many a wild ride while you were still pooping your diapers, Kidd."

Kidd and Rose were anchored at the bar. Rita, accustomed to ruling the roost as bartender/proprietor, obviously did not like being kept in the dark by her friends. To her way of thinking, such a thing was a grievous insult.

"Sorry," said Kidd. "It's just that I know how crazy it will sound to you."

"I *told* him we should ask you to go with us," said Rose, taking Rita's side.

Rita fired up a smoke and gave Kidd her dreaded dead-eye look, a non-verbal warning that said you'd best watch your step because you were treading on very thin ice.

Kidd sighed. "All right. You want the whole truth? Here it is. The Fluckers say they've found one of those urban legend roads and the reason they want me along on the return trip is because I have the unique ability of being able to see the strange creatures that run the roads. This scar under my eye? One of those monsters put it there the night my parents died in the wreck. My comings and goings you mark on your calendar? That's me lighting out to look for trocs. That's what I call them. Trocs. Because I have to call them something, and nobody else has ever seen one, as far as I know, so nobody ever gave them a name. Does that not sound like an insane load of shit to you?"

Rita smiled crookedly, venting smoke through her nostrils. "That it does," she said. "But sometimes it takes a good load of shit to make things grow. Not that *your* imagination needs much fertilizer."

"See? I knew you wouldn't believe it."

"I'd have to see it to believe it. But I believe you believe it and that's okay with me. It's like Bigfoot. Maybe he's real and maybe he's not. But until he shows his hairy ass around here, I'm not gonna lose sleep worrying if he's real or not."

"No, it's not like that," Kidd argued. "Bigfoot, according to popular lore, avoids populated areas. Trocs don't. You could be sharing the road with one on your drive home tonight and not even know it. Unless it leads you off on a stolen road and has you for supper."

"Like being fairy led," Rose interjected as if it had just now dawned on her.

Rita laughed. "I'm sorry, but that's too *out there* for me. It might make a good cheesy movie on the Sci-fi Channel but it's just flat unbelievable."

"Then come with us," said Rose. "See it and believe it."

"Have you seen one of these roads, Rose?" Rita asked.

"No, but I've seen enough weird shit to know better than to close my mind to the possibility that there's a lot of *weirder* shit out there in the Big Nowhere."

"You talking about hallucinations?"

"No. I know when I'm hallucinating. I get this tingle between my eyes when I'm seeing stuff that ain't there. And anyway, that hasn't happened in a long time. I'm all better now."

Rita nodded, her expression blank.

The jukebox started playing a raucous country and western song about a "crazy ex-girlfriend."

Kidd said, "That's the nutshell story. The Fluckers say they can take us to a lost road. Maybe they're full of shit and maybe they're not. Only one way to find out."

"I believe 'em," Rose said. "I've got a good bullshit detector and they didn't trigger it."

"So when are you going?" asked Rita.

"Day after tomorrow," he said. "When the moon is full."

Rita grinned. "This just gets better and better. I wonder if you'll meet up with a werewolf."

"There," Kidd said, pointing an accusing finger at Rita. "That's why I didn't want to confide in you. I knew you'd react like that."

"I'm sorry, Kidd. That was rude of me. I shouldn't make fun."

"Don't make fun of the loonies. That's what you're saying."

"No, no, that's not what I'm saying. I just don't like to see my friends taken advantage of. I think the Fluckers are doing a number on you. I don't know what their game is, but I know they're playing you."

"Yeah, well, we'll let you know," he said. "When we get back. For now, let's just drop it. Before somebody gets pissed."

Rita crushed her smoke in an ashtray. "I'm half tempted to go along for the ride," she said, her tone suddenly conciliatory.

"I wish you would," Rose said.

"Tell you what, Kidd," said Rita, slapping her palm on the bar. "I'll bet you a hundred bucks this whole thing is a hoax. That the Fluckers won't be taking you anywhere but down the primrose path."

"The what?" Rose queried with a scrunched-up face.

Kidd patiently explained: "It means being led astray, deceived. I think Shakespeare first coined the phrase in *Hamlet*."

"He's my walking encyclopedia on word and phrase origins," said Rose, jerking a thumb in Kidd's direction.

"How about it? You up for a friendly little bet?" Rita folded her arms and rested her elbows on the bar. She was wearing a navy sweater with a V-neck that displayed the deep cleft of her breasts.

"I don't want your money," he said. "Not that I think it's a sure bet. I'm like you. I'll believe it when I see it. But the only way to see if it's for real is to go along."

"Aw, come on. Take the bet."

Rita was needling him and he didn't like it. He decided to up the ante to see if she was bluffing. He said, "If we bet, then you'll have to go with us to see the outcome for yourself. I wouldn't expect you to pay off on the word of a lunatic alone."

Rita nodded thoughtfully. "All right, by God," she said. "You're on. I could use a little excitement for a change. A moonlight ride might be fun."

She offered her hand. Kidd shook it to seal the wager.

"Hot damn!" Rose shouted with a big grin. Then she tossed her cap high into the smoky haze.

CHAPTER EIGHT

George and Mallory Flucker arrived on schedule in their tricked-out orange Hummer. Mallory waggled her fingers at Rose and Kidd, who were leaning against Rose's pickup in front of the Hoot.

"Wow-ow-ow," Rose said, dropping her half-smoked cigarette to the gravel and stepping on it. "How cool is that!"

"An Orange Maria," said Kidd.

"What?"

"Nothing." He could've told her that a Black Maria (pronounced *Mariah*) was an antiquated nickname for a paddywagon, but he couldn't have explained why the Humvee brought it to mind. This model had a four-door cab with a boxy top, and except for the rebellious color and lack of onboard weaponry, the wide-bodied utility vehicle was true to its military origin.

The Hummer rolled to a gravel-crunching halt right in front of them.

"Climb in," George called from the driver's seat.

Rose and Kidd got in the back, and a moment later they were speeding down the road.

Turning in her seat, Mallory said, "We're going to ground zero. It's a hundred mile drive so make yourselves comfortable."

"Seems like a waste of gas, going there now," Kidd observed.

"We can afford a bit of extravagance now and then," said George.

"We inherited a fortune when my father died," Mallory explained. "He was a big-shot oil company exec. That's how we can afford to do what we do."

"Our peculiar pursuits," George said with a laugh. He was in very high spirits. "But there's a method in our madness. I want you, Kidd, to test your vision at the location. A little experiment to see if you can see anything other than an ordinary stretch of road. You can see those creatures when nobody else can, so who's to say you might not pick up on any peculiarities or anomalies before the way opens at the full of the moon? See what I mean?"

"I wouldn't get my hopes up," Kidd said.

"Even if you can't, we'll still spend the time planning our strategy."

Rose said, "We've got somebody else you should add to the team."

Kidd saw George's scowl in the rearview mirror as they turned onto the entrance ramp to the Interstate.

"We've got a full boat," George said. "We don't need anyone else."

"You know her," Rose went on, undeterred. "She runs the Hoot'n'Holler. Rita?"

George's scowl deepened, his high spirits visibly flagging. "We're not going on a picnic, you know. This is serious business."

"That's okay, coz Rita's not the picnic type. She all business. A real motorcycle mama. Tell 'em, Kidd-o."

"She would be good to have along, especially if things get hairy," said Kidd.

"We just don't have the room," George countered.

"She could drive her own truck," Kidd said. "It's not a bad idea to have an extra vehicle on the trip. Increase our chances of getting back."

After an uncomfortable silence, George said, "We don't want word of what we're doing to make the rumor-mill rounds. Discretion is vital. Whatever we may find over there, we don't want our discovery exposed by way of a tabloid media circus. We want to control the situation ourselves, in a dignified manner. Also, with two vehicles we might get separated over there. Somebody could get stranded. We just don't know."

Kidd said, "You've put a lot of thought into this, haven't you." It wasn't a question. Kidd was duly impressed by the man's grasp of the realities that were sure to surround such a startling discovery. Even if they managed to take down a troc and return with the body, they would have to take care to avoid the media sensationalism that would no doubt occur.

"Of course," said George. "I'm dead serious about how serious we are."

Rose said, "Rita's cool. You can trust her to keep a tight lip."

"Not like somebody I know," Kidd said, digging an elbow into Rose's ribs.

"Hey, if I hadn't said anything to these good peeps, you never would've met them. I know when to keep my mouth shut."

Kidd decided to lay it on the line. "If Rita doesn't go, I don't go."

"The woman seems all right to me," Mallory told her husband. "And having a second vehicle does seem like a good idea."

"Christ," said George. "I'm outnumbered."

"Let's vote on it," Rose said.

"Don't bother," George said, sulking for effect. "You've already won. She can come."

Mallory leaned over and planted a kiss on his cheek.

George shrugged. "I just don't like the feeling of losing command. I guess I fancied myself the commander of this expedition. But obviously I'm not."

"Don't pout, sugar," his wife said, half in jest. "You're still my hero."

"Please," said George, obviously embarrassed.

"You're the man with the plan," Kidd said. "Let's hear it."

"Mallory and I both did the planning. It's just common sense stuff, with an eye to things that might go wrong. Like getting stuck over there. We almost did the last time and that put the fear of the Lord in us both."

"You mentioned getting out of the vehicle and going on foot," Kidd said. "I don't think that's a good idea with trocs on the ground. It would be safer to stay in this baby."

"We'll play it by ear," he conceded. "Safety first, of course."

"I'll have to get out to get rock samples," said Rose.

"Nobody gets out if we see any trocs," Kidd said. "You said you thought you saw six last time. No way we could fight off that many."

"Have you ever seen them attack anyone?" asked George.

"No. I told you what it did to my dad when he was already dying. Once I saw one running alongside an SUV. It reached out and ripped the front tire to shreds. The driver narrowly avoided a rollover and the troc just disappeared into the road. The others I've seen were just cruising, like they were waiting for accidents to happen. Whether they'll be more aggressive on their home ground, I can't say. But they may well be."

"What do you mean, *it just disappeared into the road?*" asked Mallory.

"It looked like it passed right through the asphalt, like a ghost passing through walls. But it might've been an optical illusion on my part. I can see them but my perspective is limited. It appears that they have to obey only *some* of the laws of physics in our world. My sense of it—my intuition is that they can run in both worlds at the same time. Like one world overlaps with another for them. Which is why the notion of lost roads resonates in me. It fits what I know about trocs. Or what I think I know."

George said, "I hope they show up on any video footage we shoot. We'll have two night-vision cameras. One handheld and the other mounted on front of the Hummer. And I would like you, Rose, to chip off a sample of the road over there. A few of those eyewitness accounts describe the roads as quite different from what we're familiar with. I want to bring back a chunk and have it analyzed."

"I'm your girl," Rose agreed. "No problem."

"That's the *only* reason I can see for getting out of the vehicle," Kidd said.

"We're explorers, Kidd," George said with a note of awe in his voice. "Can't you see the symbolic importance of setting foot on unknown territory? I mean to plant a flag over there."

"A giant leap for mankind," Mallory said with considerably less awe.

Kidd thought the flag was a foolish idea, but he didn't say so. He suspected that George would feel much less adventurous in the company of trocs.

*   *   *

It was three-thirty when they turned onto Highway 136. It was a sunny afternoon and the shadows were lengthening. It was a perfect autumn day.

"It's ten miles down this road," George said. "I drove a stake in the ground to mark the spot."

Kidd stiffened his spine against the Hummer's backseat. He leaned forward for a clearer look at the road ahead.

George pulled to the road's shoulder and stopped the vehicle.

"What? Why're we stopping?" Rose asked.

"Kidd, swap seats with Mallory," said George. "I want you to have a front-row seat. In case there's something to see."

Kidd climbed out, Mallory got in the back with Rose, and Kidd took the shotgun seat.

Pulling the vehicle back on the road, George said, "Look sharp. I'll go slow. Sing out if you see anything unusual."

"Aye, aye, Skipper," said Kidd. He was beginning to see Flucker as a big kid playing out a half-assed fantasy inspired by childhood adventure stories. The impression didn't inspire confidence.

They crawled down the stretch of country road at twenty miles per hour. The compass on the dash indicated that they were traveling northeast.

"See anything?" asked impatient Rose.

"Same thing you see," Kidd said.

"No talking now," George said. "Don't distract him."

They rode the rest of the ten miles in uneasy silence. Kidd saw nothing unusual.

George again pulled over on the roadside. "Here we are. Right along here is where we began our amazing moonlight ride. There's my marker. It's not the exact spot, but it's our best estimate."

"It's definitely where we came back out," Mallory said. "I remember seeing that dead tree there and thanking the Lord that we were back on terra firma."

"She means *familiar* ground," said George. "The ground over there certainly seemed solid enough. Real enough too. Maybe more real than here."

"How so?" Kidd asked.

"It just seemed...more real. Harsher. Even in the moonlight. It's hard to explain. Maybe it was just a heightened sense of reality, altered perception. But I remember thinking at the time that the world over there was the real thing and that our regular world on this side is a pale copy of it, with less…gravitas."

"Say what?" said Rose.

"Don't mind him," Mallory said in loud whisper. "Sometimes he tries to take on a tad too much *gravitas* himself."

"That woman from Jasper said the same thing," George said. "The preacher's wife? She said she didn't like to talk about it because it was 'too real.' I know exactly what she meant."

"Me too," said Rose. "Some of my scariest hallucinations were way too real. One time I saw this guy with a little orange tree growing out his chest. Nice looking oranges too. There was this other time I had a hallucination meant for somebody else. Like there was this—"

"Not now, dear," said George. "It's time to enter the, uh, Lost Road Zone. Everybody ready?"

"Hell yeah," Rose said, quickly shifting her mental gears. "Gun it, Captain Ahab."

*   *   *

"Hear that? That humming noise?" George cocked his head to one side.

"This *is* a Hummer, dude," Rose said with a brittle laugh.

Mallory shushed her: "Listen!"

Kidd heard nothing above the usual sound of tire rubber meeting pavement and the hum of the engine.

"Guess it was my imagination," George said. "Still…"

Kidd took in the landscape. Woodland on the right, a weedy meadow on the left, then an old brick chimney where a small house had once stood. A cluster of spindly pines trees. Ordinary countryside. So why was he feeling so suddenly anxious? Why were the hairs on the back of his neck standing at attention like a displaced platoon of soldiers?

He touched a fingertip to the scar under his eye. Sometimes it itched.

It wasn't itching now, but it was tingling a little. And then there it was: a barely perceptible twitch, the tiniest tic of scarred flesh beneath his eye. A tic that told him a troc was likely in the vicinity. Trouble was, it wasn't a hundred percent reliable as troc-detecting radar. Sometimes anxiety could set off the tic. And he *was* a little anxious now, so he didn't leap to any conclusion about the presence of the beasts. What he did was move to the edge of his seat and open his eyes a little wider as he scanned the road ahead and the passing countryside, on high alert.

"What? You see something, Kidd?" George asked.

"No. Nothing yet."

George pulled a flask from his coat pocket and took a drink. He offered it to Kidd. Kidd declined. He didn't want anything to dull his senses.

"I'll take a hit," said Rose.

George passed it back to her.

Kidd kept his eyes on the road. The scar twitched again—a slight but insistent tic.

He'd first heard of lost or stolen roads from a trucker he'd hitched a ride with outside of Memphis. The talkative trucker said he'd driven many a mile of bad road but had never come across a "lost one"—though he did believe that he'd given a ride to a hitchhiking ghost one time near New Orleans. Subsequently, Kidd researched lost roads on the Internet but didn't find anything he considered credibly substantial. He had wondered then if lost or stolen roads might be linked to the seemingly random appearances of trocs, but since he'd never met anyone who claimed to have been on such a road and had never seen one himself, he soon dropped the idea and wrote off stolen roads as just another urban myth. The Internet was a breeding ground/repository for all kinds of wacky crap. Everybody knew that.

But now that he was riding into an alleged Lost Road Zone with the Fluckers as guides, he realized that he might've been too hasty in discounting the concept of ghostly roads. According to a report he'd seen on CNN, a staggering number of people went missing each year —just under one million people. How many of them might've been taken by way of a stolen road into oblivion?

He closed his eyes and pictured a maze of roads like dark arteries crisscrossing the continent, some of them capable of capturing unsuspecting motorists and taking them into a desolate land from which they might never return.

When he opened his eyes he saw movement out at the edge of his vision, on the right side of the road. He turned his head to see a shadow running along the road's shoulder. Then he saw what was making the shadow: a mangy, malnourished dog, loping along and easily keeping pace with the slow-moving Hummer. He blew a sigh of relief, realizing as he did so that he didn't want to see a troc. He didn't want this to be a lost road. What could this be but a colossal loss of nerve? He was *afraid*. He was a kid again. He was the same lost boy who'd lost his parents to a horrible accident—which may not have been an accident at all. His old psychosis tugged at him, its echo from the past calling out to him across confusing fields of time. He shook it off, disgusted with himself for letting fear get such a firm grip on his psyche.

"That's one ugly dog," Mallory said.

"Probably a hellhound," Rose observed. "Our escort to the underworld."

"George?" Mallory suddenly leaned forward to touch her husband's shoulder. "Why is the compass doing that?"

"My God," George said, "look at that."

The compass needle was sweeping counterclockwise at roughly the speed of a clock's second hand. George tapped the compass with his fingertips, to no effect. The needle continued its leftward course, seeking but not finding magnetic north.

"Is it broken?" Mallory asked.

"Can't be. It was working fine a few minutes ago. And we were heading northeast."

Rose said, "And now we're what, going in circles? What the fuck, dude?"

"An electromagnetic anomaly," George said with a smile of self-satisfaction. "An indication of unusual forces at play on this stretch of road. We shouldn't be surprised, knowing what we know."

"I'm not sure what we know but I don't think we're in Kansas anymore, Toto," Mallory said with a nervous laugh.

"We should've brought guns," Kidd said.

"Why do you say that?" asked George.

"I'm getting a bad feeling," said Kidd, absently touching his scar.

"Not to worry," said George as he reached down to his ankle, lifted the hem of his pant leg and drew a small pistol from an ankle holster. "I'm strapped, as they say. Thirty-two semiautomatic. Never leave home without it."

Kidd was unimpressed with Flucker's firepower. "What if you're wrong about the full moon? What if we're about to be taken right now?"

"You're not getting cold feet, are you?" George asked him.

Maybe I am, Kidd thought, but he said nothing. He didn't want to show fear in the face of a threat, real or imagined.

"My feet are cold all the way up to my ass," Rose said. "How about turning on the heater, Captain?"

Then Kidd glanced to the right and saw a blurred shadow-shape running behind the loping dog. He turned in his seat for a better look. His pulse accelerated. Beneath his eye, scar tissue twitched wildly.

Then the fast-moving shadow shifted into a familiar *solid* form, and Kidd gaped at the fastest troc he'd ever seen.

CHAPTER NINE

"Stop the car!" Kidd shouted.

Flucker hit the brakes and the Hummer lurched to a halt on the shoulder of the road.

"What the fuck!" Rose exclaimed.

"There!" Kidd jabbed a finger in the direction of the troc. "The dog!"

The mutt must've sensed that doom was upon it because it went from a lazy lope into an all-out four-legged sprint, tearing off down the road in front of the Hummer. But the troc was too fast; it easily caught its canine prey and took it down. It happened so quickly that all Kidd could see was a blur of fur and a flash of green-and-black pebbled skin, and then a splash of blood. The troc and the dog disappeared into the blacktop.

"Holy shit," said Rose, who had leaned up from the backseat to peer over George Flucker's shoulder. "Where'd it go?"

"My God," said Mallory. "It just vanished."

"Did you see it? Did anybody see the troc?" Kidd turned excitedly to his companions.

"I think I saw something," George said, "but it happened too fast. You *saw* one?"

"Yeah. A small one. But I saw it clearly."

"That's not possible," Mallory said in a shaky voice. "A dog can't just disappear like that."

"But it did," Kidd said. "All that's left is blood on the road."

George threw open the door and jumped out of the vehicle with the petite pistol in his fist. "Let's have a closer look."

"No! Get back in here right now, George," his wife said sharply.

Kidd opened his door as he said, "I think it's all right. It's gone for now."

"But it could come back," Mallory said.

"We'll just be a minute," Kidd said. He got out and walked briskly to catch up with George.

They stood ten yards in front of the Hummer and stared at the spatter of blood on the blacktop. There was a fist-size clump of black fur in the center of the gore.

"Unbelievable," said George. He pulled his flask out of his tan jacket and took a big gulp of its contents, then he handed it to Kidd. "Scotch."

Kidd took a swallow. It burned pleasantly going down.

"Nobody would ever believe what we just saw. Damn, I wish I'd gone ahead and mounted the video camera on the Hummer. I didn't think we'd see anything this trip And I didn't want to tempt thieves."

"This is the first time I've seen one attack anything living." Kidd looked around to be sure there were no other trocs in the area. In the *visible* area. "Except my dad, and he was already dying. And it didn't really attack him so much as it sucked the last breath of life from him."

George took another pull from his flask and said, "It took that poor mutt right out of the world. Bloody fucking amazing."

A sudden blast of noise made both men jump. Mallory had honked the Hummer's horn. "Get in the car!" she shouted.

George gave her a cursory nod and waved her off as if swatting at an annoying gnat. "Well, we know where it took the hound," he said. "Into the land of lost roads. You know what this means, don't you, Kidd? It's confirmation that the world isn't as solid as everybody thinks it is. Reality isn't as *real* as we like to believe. This world has a very thin skin indeed."

*   *   *

They rode ten more miles down the road without incident. The GPS signal ghosted in and out but never disappeared altogether. The entire time they'd been on the troc-haunted stretch of road, there had been no other traffic, which prompted George to speculate that perhaps the locals instinctively avoided it. Mallory said she thought they should cancel the full-moon ride because of what had happened to the dog.

"Makes me think twice about getting out of the vehicle," George conceded, "but we can't call off the expedition. Great discoveries often go hand-in-hand with danger. No, dear, we can't beg off now. We *have* to go through with it. Right, Kidd?"

"Yes, but maybe the ladies shouldn't."

"You're calling me a lady now?" Rose slapped the back of his seat. "Ha!"

"Do you know how sexist that sounded?" Mallory asked him.

"But you just said—"

"If anybody goes, *I'm* going."

"Well done, son," George said out of the corner of his mouth. "You're a master manipulator."

"I heard that," Mallory said with an edge of angry warning in her voice.

George chortled as he turned the Hummer around in the middle of the road and headed back the way they'd come.

"Wonder what those things feed on where they come from?" asked Rose. "You know, like do they run down monster rabbits or something or do they have to come over to our side to find food?"

"I was wondering the same thing," said Mallory.

"What do you think, Kidd?" George asked.

"I can't imagine a world with only one species of animal. It just doesn't make sense, given the laws of nature. But it may be that the pickings are better here."

"Once you get a taste for people meat, I guess it's hard to go back," Rose said with a hollow laugh.

Kidd said, "We don't know for a fact that they actually eat human flesh. The one that gave me this" —he touched his scar— "didn't eat me or my parents. I've never been able to shake the idea that it was trying to eat my father's soul. Or just reveling in death itself, like it was sort of a religious ritual to watch a man die."

"It sure snatched the holy shit out of that poor mutt's ass," Rose said.

"Maybe they're such good hunters that they've depleted their natural food supply, like our buffalo hunters in the late eighteen hundreds,"

George suggested. "We won't really know until somebody goes on an extended expedition over there. Someday, a modern Lewis & Clark will have to go exploring and map whatever's there. Following our lead, of course."

"I wouldn't mind going along with them," Rose said, "except for the part about being troc food. Or sacramental booty."

Mallory said, "If this ever gets written up as one of the world's great discoveries, we'll probably rate a fat footnote."

"If we play our cards right," said George, "we'll rate a whole chapter."

"That's if we don't get stuck over there, never to be heard from again," said Mallory.

*   *   *

When Flucker's marker—a short wooden stake with a red-and-blue flowered scarf tied to it—came into view, the compass needle ceased its erratic sweep and finally found north. Rose was the one who first noticed it, saying, "Check it out. The compass came back from Crazy Town."

"Back to familiar reality," said George.

"I've still got goose bumps," Mallory said. "And a sick dread in the pit of my stomach. That poor dog. That was just so wrong."

Kidd had a knot of dread in his belly too, though not exactly for the same reason. As the Hummer pulled even with Flucker's road marker, he voiced his concern. "Why did the troc do that right in front of us? They must know people can't see them when they slip into our world, yet this one made a spectacle of what they can do to a dog. They're too cunning to give so much away without good reason."

"So what would that reason be?" asked George.

"I think it was daring us," Kidd said. "It was a challenge."

"What, daring us to go after it?" Mallory asked him.

"Maybe."

"Like it wants to lure our asses onto its home turf," Rose said. "Maybe they already know what we're up to and the bit with the dog was to poke a big finger in our eyes."

"I wouldn't invest them with clairvoyance," George cautioned. "That sort of wild speculation won't do us any good. How could they possibly know what's in our minds? They may have abilities that to us seem supernatural, but I promise you they are not omniscient."

Kidd shrank into his seat. Should he tell them? Should he confide in his old mental-hospital mate and these two relative strangers that he sometimes feared that the trocs were tracking him? Should he confess that he sometimes believed the beasts knowingly showed themselves to him as part of a road-running game of cat-and-mouse? That he half believed they had plans for him?

Then hailstones began to fall from the clear autumn sky, overruling any thoughts of confession. The stones were small at first, pea-size pellets of ice clattering on the Hummer's roof and bonnet. Within a matter of seconds, the pelting hailstones were bigger than golf balls, and George floored the gas pedal, lest the freak hailstorm damage the vehicle.

"Holy shit," Rose shouted over the noisy clatter.

The Hummer shot down the road, and half a minute later they were out of the storm.

"Curiouser and curiouser," said Mallory

"Don't look now," said Rose, "but I think we're already down the rabbit hole."

CHAPTER TEN

Though Kidd wasn't accustomed to thinking this way, he was beginning to believe that everything that had happened since his most recent arrival back at the Hoot and homebase had been preordained by forces about which he knew next to nothing.

From the Fluckers' calling card left at the bar and the arrival of Rose Rivers, to their preliminary ride on the lost road and into the freak hailstorm—it was all meant to happen, meant to unfold just so, all of it plotted out in advance and leading to some inevitable, unimaginable conclusion. This sort of thinking rankled. It flew in the face of his belief in free will. It made him want to run away, to hit the road and wander aimlessly, to forget all about trocs and stolen roads and slaughtered dogs.

But he was not the sort to turn tail and run. In a sense, he *was* a chosen one. Rose had been right about that. Call it destiny if you like, but he could no more run from his calling than he could run from the scar on his cheek. He was very much in the game and he had no choice but to play it out to the end. Win or lose, Kidd was destined to be in the thick of the action—no matter how bizarrely coming events might unfold.

"You look like somebody just shot your dog and pissed in your beer," Rita told him when she came down to his end of the bar.

"I never had a dog," said Kidd, surfacing from the shallows of his thoughts. "And if there's piss in the beer, that's your problem."

"Boy, you're a grumpy Humphrey. What's the matter? Did your outing with the Fluckers turn to shit? "

"More like blood and hail," he said.

"Don't go all cryptic on me, Kidd. What happened?"

He told her about the troc attack on the dog and about the hailstorm. Then he said, "If you don't want to go, I'll let you out of our bet."

"I never welsh on a bet, Kidd," she said, giving him a stern look. "You know, I'm almost beginning to believe all this stuff. You're so damned convincing."

"You need to believe it. It's real."

Rita shook out one of her Virginia Slims and lit it. "Where's Rose?"

"Exploring your mountain," Kidd said with a shrug. "Looking for magic rocks behind the Hoot."

"That girl's a hoot herself. You really know how to pick 'em, Kidd."

"She sort of picked me, I think."

"Fate threw you together."

"Yeah, I guess."

"She's a sweet kid once you get to know her."

He nodded, then asked, "Where's a good place to shoot a gun around here? For target practice."

"You have a gun?"

"The Fluckers gave them to us. A rifle and pistol."

Rita blew smoke at the ceiling. "Have you ever fired a gun?"

He shook his head. "My dad got rid of his guns when it became clear that his son was a nutcase."

"I know *you're* okay now, but is it wise to put a deadly weapon in Rose's hands?"

"I think she's stable enough. Her rock hammer could be a dangerous weapon, so could her truck, but she's never hurt anybody."

"The Fluckers just give you the guns and expect you to teach yourselves how to shoot? I don't know about those two. I'm having serious doubts, you know?" She took a thoughtful drag on her Slim. "Tell you what. I'll teach you and Rose how to shoot. First thing in the morning."

"I was going to ask if you would. Thanks, Rita."

She took another drag, leaned closer to him over the bar and said, "Nothing left but blood and the hair of the dog, huh?"

He nodded.

"And the dog just disappeared into the road." Her expression was grave.

"I know it's incredible but that's what happened. We all saw it."

"But you're the only one who saw the croc."

"Troc," he corrected her.

"Unbelievable."

"I know."

"But I know you're not pulling my leg. I know you're serious as cancer."

He nodded once more.

"This is what gives me the heebie-jeebie creeps. That you're so damned serious about it."

"It's a creepy concept," he said. "This world—" Kidd rapped his knuckles on the bar—"overlaps with one totally foreign to us. And beasts from that world have learned how to come into ours, to hunt."

"To hunt us."

"So it appears."

"And we're gonna saddle up and ride right into their world and hunt them."

"Well, something like that. But I wouldn't exactly call it a hunting expedition. It's an exploration. If it works and we actually can cross over. The Fluckers say they've done it and they're confident we can do it again."

"And this has been going on how long?"

"The first known report of a lost road was in 1945, according to the Fluckers."

Rita furrowed her brow. "The same year the first atomic bombs went off, right?"

He waited for her to finish her thought.

"You think..." She broke off to wait on a new customer at the far end of the bar. She left her cigarette smoking in the ashtray. Kidd waved the smoke out of his face and waited for her to come back.

He looked at his reflection in the long mirror behind the bar. The reflecting glass was marbled, his image fragmented and dim. The scar under his eye seemed to shine with otherworldly light. He shut his eyes and went away. A feeling of dislocation lifted him off the barstool and set him adrift between worlds. He opened his eyes and for a fraction of a second he wasn't in the mirror. And then he was, and he reached for Rita's cigarette and took a hit, inhaling deeply. The smoke made him light-headed but the cigarette kept him here, moored him to the smoky world.

Rita was her own woman, a free spirit if ever there was. She was living proof of free will. Wasn't she? It wasn't her cigarette keeping him here—it was Rita. He needed her. He set the cigarette back in the ashy groove.

Then she was in front of him again, the cigarette between her fingers. "So what if those atomic explosions back in forty-five did something…I don't know, blew holes, in what? Reality? And opened our world to this other one. Like holes in the ozone but opening up these roads. Lost roads."

"And all those fifties science-fiction movies were right," he said, fixing on her face. "About playing God, messing with Mother Nature. It looses monsters upon the world."

Rita laughed. But it sounded hollow, not her usual chest-and-belly laugh. "There's monsters," she said, "and then there's *monsters*. It's the human ones you got to watch out for."

"Rita…"

She looked expectantly at him.

"We might not come back from over there. You need to know that."

She crushed her cigarette in the ashtray and squinted against the smoke.

Kidd said, "I don't want anything to happen to you. I'm glad you're going, but…I don't want to lose you."

She reached over the bar and squeezed his hand. "Don't worry about me, babe. I'm going along because I don't wanna lose you. And I don't do one-way trips."

"I don't want you to lose me either," he said in total honesty.

"No way in hell," she said, cocking one brow and squeezing his hand harder.

He wanted to tell her she was like family but his throat was too constricted with emotion to get the words out. Then she was looking over his shoulder, smiling. "*¿Qué pasa, Manuel?*"

Manuel Cervantes sat on the stool next to Kidd and said, "I got her running. She's all tuned up and chomping at the bit. Ready to ride." He pulled two cigars from his shirt pocket and gave one to Rita. "Sorry, Kidd, I don't have one for you."

Rita grinned and said, "Fantastic! Thanks, man. Perfect timing, eh, Kidd? I'd say that's a damn good omen."

Kidd wanted to tell her a motorcycle was too dangerous, that it would almost certainly invite a troc attack, but he didn't want to spoil the moment so he said nothing.

*   *   *

Rose wasn't back before dark and Kidd was beginning to worry. She had said she would meet him here for a bowl of Rita's infamously spicy-hot chili and a few brews. Thinking that she might've gone back to his place for a shower first, he drank another beer and waited, trying not to worry. That was the trouble with getting close to people. The more you came to care about a person, the more you worried for their safety. This was the reason Kidd endeavored to be a loner. He knew how quickly you could lose everything. He knew how tenuous life truly was. But no matter how hard he tried, he couldn't be the lone wolf, not for any significant length of time. For all his man-alone-on-the-road posturing, he was, at heart, the proverbial babe in the woods.

Manuel had gone home to his wife and kids, and Rita was on the phone, talking to Weeda, her good friend and part-time employee, to arrange for coverage at the roadhouse on the night of the full-moon ride. The jukebox was playing Johnny Cash. The Hoot was drawing a good crowd tonight. Kidd was having one of those moments of feeling achingly alone in a roomful of people.

"I just had a whatchamacallit," Rose said over his shoulder, her lips brushing his ear, "an epiphany."

Kidd did a quarter turn on the stool, reached out and pulled her into a crushing hug.

"Whoa, dude. Is that a rod in your pants or are you just glad to see me?"

"The guns are back at the crib," he said, "and I *am* glad to you see you."

She laughed. Her cap was sitting sideways on her head, the bill hanging over her left ear. There was a smudge of dirt on the side of her jaw. She mounted the barstool and spun a full circle.

"I was getting worried about you," he admitted. "Thought I'd been stood up."

"Sweet. Maybe now you'll sleep with me."

"I slept with you last night."

"But we didn't *do* it. Unless I slept through it. Which I would never do."

"I'm your blood brother. I don't think we're allowed to *do it*."

"I'm just yanking your chain, bro."

"Tell me about your epiphany."

Rose eagerly nodded. She removed her cap and plopped it on the bar. "I was back there on your little mountain, wandering lonely as a clod, yuck-yuck, and trying to get closer to the trees because, you know, trees are sacred, especially pine and cedar, and I don't wanna be strictly a rock person, and then I get the feeling something is following me, tracking me, something big but real quiet, stealthy as a motherfucker. So I get scared, thinking *troc*. But I'm not about to show fear so I sit under a pine and say a Cherokee purification prayer. '*Great spirit Unequa, whose voice I hear in the wind, whose breath gives life to all the world, hear me: I need your strength and wisdom. Let me walk in beauty, and make my eyes ever behold the red and purple sunset. Help me to remain calm and strong in the face of all that comes toward me. Let me learn the lessons you have hidden in every leaf and rock. Make me always ready to come to you with clean hands and straight eyes. So when life fades, as the fading sunset, my spirit may come to you without shame.*' I left a lot of it out but that was all I could remember. It was enough, 'cause whatever was stalking me went away. I felt it leave. And then an owl hoots and I know I'm okay. The owl being sacred to the Cherokee."

"Good," said Kidd. "That's good."

"Wait, I'm not done. Then the owl spoke to me. He told me that where we're going there aren't many trees to shelter his brothers but that it didn't matter because the spirit can travel easily in all the worlds and in the seven directions."

"Seven? I only know of four."

Rose shrugged. "I'm telling you what he told me. If Brother Owl says seven, then that's how many there are."

"So, did the owl speak English?" He gave her a cockeyed look.

"No, numbnuts. It spoke *hoot*. But I knew what he was saying coz he's a magical animal, and I was wearing my medicine bag. He was saying they would be looking out after us over there in Troc Land. Protecting us. Which I was happy as shit to hear because I don't mind telling you, I was getting really freaked about going. But now it's cool. *I'm* cool. Now how about that chili? I'm starving my narrow ass off."

*   *   *

The night had turned cold. He turned on the small space heater and waited for it to heat the air inside his cinderblock living quarters. Rose was in the shower, a steamy little lodge of wet warmth. Good medicine.

She came out wearing nothing but a white towel, her mop of hair toweled half-dry and wild. "If you're gonna take one, wait awhile. I used up all the hot water." She stood in front of the boxy little heater. The towel wasn't big enough to cover much of her nakedness.

"That wasn't an epiphany you had," he said.

"Then what the hell was it? And don't say hallucination."

"You heard an owl. Your imagination made up the message you needed to hear to control your fear."

"No, White Eyes. You think that because you don't believe in spiritual beings. You believe in your trocs but not in nature spirits. You're the one who's weird. Not me."

"I didn't say you're weird."

"You've got troc spit in your blood, I've got Cherokee blood in me. Deal with it, as they used to say in group therapy."

Kidd shrugged. "Maybe you're right. Maybe it was a divine manifestation. That's not the point. I just don't want any of us to be overconfident. We *should* be afraid. Fear is a healthy thing. It can make you careful and keep you alive. Don't rely on mystical spirits to protect you. Do it yourself."

"I hear you," she said, dropping the towel. She placed his hands on her breasts.

"Rose…"

Her nipples felt frisky against his palms.

"I lied," he said in a hoarse whisper. "I am a virgin."

"You serious?"

He nodded.

"Why'd you lie?"

"I dunno. So I wouldn't have to explain it, I guess."

"Explain it now." She fondled his erection through his jeans.

"I think I'm supposed to wait."

"Wait for what?" she asked, breathless.

"I don't know. I just know I'm supposed to."

She pulled away. "So we're not…?"

He shook his head. "I'll take a walk, if you want to…you know."

"No, dude. I'll wait for the real thing."

"Sorry."

"A virgin," she said with a small laugh. "Wow. Like you're some kind of holy man or something? Holy fuck, dude!"

"No, nothing like that."

"Does this have something to do with your trocs?"

"No. I don't think so."

"Yes it does. That's it, isn't it? Sure as hell."

"I'm going for a walk," he said. "To cool off."

"You know what? If it was Rita standing here instead of me, you wouldn't turn her down. I've seen the way you look at her. I know I'm not much to look at, but jeez…"

"Not true. You felt how much I wanted you."

"You're a guy. A knothole would give you a hard-on."

"Be back in a little while,' he said, opening the door.

"Okay, bro. Watch your ass. Mine sure didn't do much for you."

CHAPTER ELEVEN

Rita lined up twenty empty beer bottles on a long plank supported by two sawhorses. An embankment of ocher earth served as backstop. She came toward them, the pistol holstered low-slung on her right hip giving her a sexy swagger.

"You go first, Kidd," she said. "Remember what I said about squeezing the trigger. Don't jerk it. Caress it like you would a woman."

Rose sniggered. Kidd cut his eyes at her and she covered her mouth with her hand and made goofy eyes.

Kidd assumed the shooter's stance Rita had taught them when they first arrived here in the unpopulated hollow ten miles from the Hoot. They had spent ten or fifteen minutes dry-firing and learning the stance. Now they were ready for live fire.

"Start with the bottle on the right and work your way left, reloading as necessary," Rita instructed. "Smooth and methodical, don't rush your shot. See the shot before you take it. Muzzle to target. Then squeeze. Recoil. New target. Stay centered in your stance. Control your breathing and shoot between breaths. Ready?"

He nodded.

"Start shooting."

He sighted down the barrel of the Colt .45 George Flucker had given him. Acquired the target, held his breath and fired. The first bottle exploded.

"Good," Rita said. "Keep firing."

"Beginner's luck," Rose muttered.

Kidd took his second shot and missed. Fired again at the same bottle and blew the neck off the bottle. After the fourth hit he began to gain confidence. He emptied one clip, ejected it, then snapped in a new one. It took four clips to hit all twenty targets.

"Not bad," Rita said with her hands on her hips. "Your turn, Rose."

The morning sun was burning off the mist lingering in the hollow. The new line of bottles glinted in sunlight. Rose stepped up to the firing line Rita had scratched in the earth with the heel of her boot. The gun looked too big for Rose's hand but years of wielding a rock hammer had made her strong, and she brandished the weapon with surprising aplomb, in the end proving herself a better shot than Kidd.

"A natural-born shooter," Rita decreed. "Now let's see how good you are with a rifle."

She showed them how to handle the Remington 7600. She explained that it was a pump-action deer rifle that fired .30-06 caliber ammo, a good big-game rifle that allowed for rapid follow-up shots. She showed them how to work the slide and how to snug it against the shoulder and where to place the hands for maximum control and precision of shot. She fired it three times in rapid succession, knocking down three beer bottles. Then she handed it to Kidd and turned him loose on the firing line.

His ears were still ringing from the concussions of the heavy-caliber pistol, and he wished he'd thought to stuff his ears with something before coming here to shoot. He aimed the Remington, and Rita corrected his stance. Then he commenced firing. He quickly found that the rifle was easier to control than the pistol, his shooting more accurate.

Rose didn't do as well with the rifle as she'd done with the .45, but Rita said she was satisfied that Rose was sufficiently proficient with the deer rifle.

Kidd smiled and said he would be the rifleman and that Rose would be the *pistolero*.

"*Sí señor*," Rose said with an ersatz Spanish accent. "Now let's ride back to the cantina and raise a leetle hell, *por favor*."

*   *   *

Kidd was sandwiched between them in Rose's pickup, Rita riding shotgun with the window down and her arm propped on the seatback. The rushing air was pleasantly cool and sun-scented. He felt safe here, between them, but he knew it was little more than illusion. It reminded him of sitting between his parents at the time of their fatal accident. (He wondered for the thousandth time why his parents hadn't made him sit seatbelt-secured that night but he knew the answer: They made him sit between them so he couldn't make a psycho jump out of the moving vehicle.) There was some measure of safety in being armed with foreknowledge and in being armed with guns, but safety was a relative thing—no one was ever completely free of danger. Disaster could strike anytime, from unexpected directions. Anything could happen to anyone.

Rita was telling them tales from her past deer-hunting adventures but Kidd wasn't really listening. He was thinking ahead to tomorrow night, imagining himself shooting a troc from the shotgun seat of the Hummer. This line of thought led him to a reexamination of his motives. Why had he spent the past few years trying to track trocs? Was he after justice? Was he simply seeking to avenge his parents' deaths? Did it come down to killing those beastly interlopers for revenge? Was it that simple? That primitive?

He didn't want to think so. He wanted to believe his ongoing quest was meant to be one of discovery, driven by natural curiosity. But he couldn't shake the feeling that destiny was preparing a big surprise for him, that he'd been marked for reasons he couldn't begin to imagine.

Rose elbowed him in the ribs. "You still with us, Kidd-O?"

"Huh? Yeah, no, I'm right here."

"Well?"

"Well what?"

Rose sighed. "I asked you if you'll get out with me when I hop out of the Hummer to chip off a sample of the road. I know George will but I don't think I trust him to watch my back. He'll probably be too busy with his camera or planting his fucking flag. I want my blood brother to have my back."

"Sure. You know I will."

"You forgetting I'll be there on my bike?" Rita asked.

Rose said, "I know. And I'm really glad but Kidd's got *troc vision.*

If those scaly fuckers are around, he'll be the first to know it."

"Troc vision," said Rita, shaking her head and smiling. "What've I gotten myself into with you two?"

"Oh I don't know," said Rose, returning something like a smile, "the ride of your life?"

*   *   *

The Fluckers showed up unannounced at noon. They ambled into the Hoot, found Kidd, Rose and Rita staked out at the bar, and joined them. Mallory flashed a big grin and said, "Let's do lunch."

"Naked?" Kidd said, alluding to their email handle.

"We thought we should formerly introduce ourselves to the newest member of our team," George said with a smile and an affable nod to Rita, who was puffing on a Slim behind the bar. He offered his hand across the mahogany and said, "George Flucker. And this is my better half, Mallory."

Rita shook his hand, then Mallory's. "Rita Younger," she said.

"Pleasure," said George. "Welcome aboard. You think you could take a break from your bartending duties so we can go over our action plan? It won't take long."

"Sure," said Rita. "We can use the corner booth. You folks want lunch, it's on the house."

"That would be great," Mallory said, touching the brim of her cowboy hat. "Thank you, Rita."

"I would love one of your Hillbilly Burgers," said George.

"Me too," Mallory said. "All the way."

"Me three," said Rose.

"Nothing for me," Kidd said.

"Heck," Rita barked to her short-order cook, "walk three Billy Burgers through the garden. A greasy cheese for me."

Heck Reynolds nodded his bullet-bald head and said, "Three BBs and a cheese, coming up."

"Don't you want something?" Rita asked Kidd. "On me."

"No thanks. I'm fasting today."

"Uh-oh, this is getting serious," Rose said. "Fasting…?"

Kidd didn't try to explain himself. The truth was, he wasn't sure why he felt the need to fast. He suspected that it grew out of an impulse to purify himself for the journey ahead. This was how he'd come to think of what George called the expedition: *the journey*. But it was a journey begun long ago when his parents' car left the road and crashed at the bottom of a grassy embankment. An otherworldly creature marked the beginning of Kidd's journey with the flick of a claw, in a baptism in blood, and Kidd had been on a dark road ever since, chasing some hazy sense of destiny.

"Leave him alone," Rita told Rose. "He's got his reasons, even if we don't know what they are."

"Hear, hear!" said George. "We want the lad in good fighting trim and finely tuned. If that means fasting, then so be it."

"I could do with some fasting myself," Mallory said, "but I'm too much of a sensualist to break off my love affair with fatty food."

"I wouldn't want you any other way, dear," George said with a sly wink.

They seated themselves in the roomy horseshoe-shaped booth in the corner. Kidd once again found himself between Rita and Rose, and again he felt as if he were little more than a passive chess piece, manipulated by an unseen hand—the hand of an omnipotent entity playing out a mysterious strategy Kidd couldn't comprehend.

George launched right into the briefing while they waited for their plates to arrive. "The moon becomes full after midnight tomorrow at 12:52 a.m., so we'll want to be at the starting point no later than half past the hour. That'll give us time to make sure everything is shipshape and ready to go and time to correct any of those little things that always seem to go wrong just at the worst possible and last moment."

"What if it rains?" Rose interrupted.

"If it does, it does. That won't affect the phase of the moon. Worst case, it could limit visibility. But the weather report calls for clear skies."

"Clear and cool," Mallory added, "so everybody dress warm."

Kidd noticed an amused expression on Rita's face and he thought she must be biting her tongue to keep from openly mocking this little gathering of gullible adults. It was the same expression one might wear while listening to "true" ghost stories. He wanted to grab her and shake her and tell her not to take this expedition—this journey—too lightly.

"Now when zero hour comes," Flucker continued, "we'll start down the road, accelerating until we get up to sixty miles an hour. That's how fast we were going a month ago when we…crossed over. Speed may not be a key factor but since we aren't sure, we'll do just like last time."

Then George looked at Rita and asked, "What will you be driving?"

"A Harley," she said with pride. "A vintage nineteen-seventy-eight Lowrider."

"Good Lord," George said, his eyebrows shooting up into an irregular arch. "A motorcycle?"

"Damn straight," Rita said with annoyed obstinacy. "What of it?"

"You know about those…creatures?"

"Kidd's creepy-crawly monsters? Yeah, I know."

"But you don't believe," George said.

"I'll believe it when I see one."

"Trust me, they are real. We saw what one did to a dog." George shuddered.

"Hon," Mallory said to Rita, "you don't want to go where we're going on the back of a motorcycle. You'd be too exposed. Don't you have a car?"

"I've got a truck but I'm taking my bike. Don't waste your time trying to talk me out of it."

After a long moment of uneasy silence, Rita added, "I can ride rings around that ugly hulk you're driving. If all you say is true, my bike's maneuverability will give me an edge you won't have. I know how to ride and shoot too."

"Really," said George.

"Really," Rita affirmed. "Back in the day, I won the MC's trophy in the Ride & Shoot competition."

"I didn't know they had such things," he admitted.

"The outfit I rode with did." Rita raised an arm and pointed at a bronze statuette on a shelf behind the bar. The trophy depicted a mounted biker aiming a pistol. "There it sits."

"Cool," said Rose, duly awed by Rita's bygone triumph. "You really are my hero, ya know."

Rita cut her eyes at Rose, then reached for her cigarettes, shook one out of the pack and lit it.

George looked across the table at Rita and said, "Well, all I can say then is Godspeed."

"You don't have to say anything," she told him, poking out her lower lip to blow smoke upward over the table. "You're not responsible for me. I'm my own woman."

Smiling weakly, George nodded. "Indeed you are."

By the time their food came, Flucker had finished going over his "action plan" and was apparently satisfied that everyone was more or less on the same page. Kidd didn't think it was much of a plan. It boiled down to shooting footage with the night-vision video camera and with the one mounted on the dash, having Rose gather rock samples from the road and the landscape, plotting the longitude and latitude with the GPS (if possible, and if there was no atmospheric or multipath error that the device couldn't correct), and being alert to the danger of a possible troc attack. "The main thing," George had said, "is to make sure we come back from over there, with whatever data we can gather." After some debate, it was agreed that Rita would ride her beloved bike behind the Hummer into "Never-Never Land," as she called it.

Kidd drank iced tea while the others eagerly devoured their greasy food. Rose said it would be great if they actually "bagged one of those troc bastards" and brought it back as proof of where they'd been.

"If I see one," said Rita, "I'll kill it for you."

"Odds are, we'll see more than one," Kidd said. "Bring plenty of bullets."

Rose suddenly stiffened her spine and sat ramrod straight. "Uh-oh, Rita. Look who's here."

Rita looked, then straight away got up and walked toward the burly man standing just inside the entrance, his ballcap in his hand. It was the same man whose hand she'd smashed with the baseball bat, and now his injured hand sported a cast.

Rose gleefully told the Fluckers about the way Rita had fended off the man's drunken bar-crawling advances.

"He doesn't look drunk now," George said. "She may need some help with that moose."

"Nah," Rose said. "She can handle him. Just watch."

They all watched. The man towered over Rita by at least a foot, and he outweighed her by well over a hundred pounds, but she stood right up to him, showing no fear. They talked in low tones for a couple of minutes, and then the big man nodded his bulbous head and held out his uninjured hand. Rita gave it a shake and the man gave a deferential bow, turned on his heels and departed, shoulders slumped in humility.

"What did he want?" Rose asked when Rita returned to the booth.

"He wanted to apologize for showing his ass. He begged me not to blackball him, so I told him I'd give him one more chance."

"Most admirable," said George, whose wide-eyed expression made it unmistakably obvious that he'd gained a new appreciation of Rita's real-world capabilities. "Most admirable, indeed!"

CHAPTER TWELVE

"You mind if I sleep with you again tonight?" Kidd asked.

Rose grinned. "Does the pope poop in rosewater?"

"I'm sure I don't know."

"Hell yes he does." Her expression suddenly turned severe. "Should I be getting my hopes up or are you just being a first-class twat-teaser again?"

"No," he said. "No to both. I want to sleep close to your stone again. Share a pillow with you."

"I thought you didn't really believe that stuff."

"There *may* be something to it," he conceded. "I find it hard to believe it has actual mystical powers but it may help to focus one's dream, sort of like hypnotic suggestion."

"My stone is your stone." Then with a mischievous glint in her eyes, she added, "Even if your stones aren't mine."

*   *   *

He lies dreaming at the base of a great phallic monolith of dark roughhewn stone. Rita sits naked in the saddle of a motorcycle, its engine growling like a ferocious beast. He knows he is dreaming her, yet he knows she is truly there before him, knows that she has the power to enter effortlessly into his dreams, that she might easily beguile him with her brazen naked beauty and conduct him through swells and crevices of sensuous landscapes of flesh and bone, down narrow twisting pathways leading inevitably to earthy illumination and on into deepest mysteries of creation. Her handsome face is unreadable. Her eyes are ethereal, shining with moonlight. The spokes are dripping blood as if the wheels have just passed through a battlefield blood puddle. The bike is balanced between her long legs, her right foot resting on the ground, her slender hip cocked.

"Climb on," she says. Her nakedness makes the invitation inescapably suggestive.

He rises out of sticky moon-shadows and sleepwalks toward the virtual Godiva on the bike, leaving his body in deep slumber beneath the black monolith. This isn't the first time he's been in two places at once; as a teen his psychosis often divided him in two.

"Where's Rose?" he asks.

"Lost. Get on. They're coming up fast behind."

He climbs on the back of the bike and holds onto her smooth hips.

"Hold tight," she says over her silvery shoulder.

With a roar the bike shoots forward, its headlight cutting a dim path in the obstinate darkness.

He clings tightly to her, his dream-flesh pressing against her welcoming warmth. He slips his hands under her armpits and finds the lush firmness of her breasts.

Though she is in his hands, in a larger sense he is in hers. And for now that is enough as they speed across the rocky landscape, buffeted by evil winds.

*   *   *

"Dude, what the fuck?"

Rose hooked an elbow in his ribs. He came out of the dream with a lurch and sat up in the bed. The room was thick with night.

"You wrestling gators in your sleep?" Rose asked.

"Dreaming," he mumbled. "A dream within a dream. I was sleeping beside this pillar of dark stone, dreaming I was on the back of Rita's bike. Things were chasing us, I think."

"Where was I?"

"I don't know."

"Figures," she said with derision. "You're in love, Kiddo. You've got it bad."

"If you hadn't woken me up, I might've learned something useful."

"Yeah, like how to pop your cherry between the legs of your beloved while yours are forked over a Harley. You really need to get laid, dude. Your hormones are skewing your dreams. The dream stone could show you the biggest secret of the universe and you'd miss it because of your dimwitted dick."

His bladder was uncomfortably full but he waited for his erection to flag before getting up to go the bathroom.

"Maybe you're right," he said, waiting for what felt like a very long time.

*   *   *

They slept till nine. If Kidd had done any more dreaming, he couldn't remember it. Rose said her dreams were duds, meaning her revered stone hadn't revealed anything relevant. "I was alone in the Big Nowhere," she said, "bored shitless. What the hell does *that* mean?"

Kidd didn't offer an opinion. He thought it would serve no purpose to tell her that she'd been "lost" in his dream. He didn't want to plant a seed of fear that might grow into a self-fulfilled prophecy.

Rose drove to the Waffle House for breakfast and Kidd stayed behind, not wishing to break his fast. He was web-fishing for new information about lost or stolen roads when Manuel knocked on his door. Rather than invite him in, Kidd stepped outside to take some of the crisp autumn air. A beer truck was parked behind the Hoot, and a deliveryman was stacking cases of beer on his hand truck.

"Keed, what the hell are you up to? Rita's all mysterious about some kind of moonlight ride you're going on."

"I don't know what to tell you," Kidd said. "That's between you and Rita."

"Ain't like her to be so tightlipped. Last time I looked, there weren't any ships around here for loose lips to sink."

Kidd said nothing.

"This is something to do with your little chica Rosita, right? The strange one?"

"It's Rose, and she's not my girl. She's a friend."

"You sleep with all your friends?" Manuel's eyes sparkled with humor.

"Sleep is all we do."

Manuel shrugged. "She shows up and strange things start happening."

"Strange things were happening before she showed up. What things are you talking about?"

"Just little things that don't mean much until you start adding them up."

"What did Rita tell you?"

"Only that you all are going on some hush-hush midnight ride because of a bet she made with you. I think she wouldn't say more because she didn't want to betray your confidence."

"Then I don't guess she'll mind if I tell you what's up. Have you ever heard of lost roads? Stolen roads?"

Manuel shook his head. "Enlighten me."

Kidd told him about the roads, hitting the highlights but leaving out any mention of trocs or his own singular abilities.

"So," Manuel said when Kidd was done, "Rita is betting you won't find a lost road. Sounds like a sucker bet to me, Keed."

"How's that?"

"My money would be on you. If anybody can get lost in America, it's you and Rose." He grinned, then added, "Mexico has many stolen roads. You could even say Mexico is a stolen country, amigo."

"The lost roads I'm talking about have nothing to do with geopolitics."

"And everything to do with phantasmagoria. I get it, man. And I hope you find what you've been looking for so long." Manuel's expression turned thoughtful. "I hope you don't find any of those *bestias* like the ones in your drawings."

With those words, Manuel departed, leaving Kidd to ponder his friend's acute powers of perception.

*   *   *

Rose returned from breakfast and made a show of taking her medication. "Just so you know," she told Kidd, "that I'm properly medicated and not batshit crazy when the real shit goes down."

"Which shit would that be?"

"Whatever shit we get into down the road to the Big Nowhere. If I see some crazy shit it won't be because *I'm* crazy." She recapped her plastic pill bottle and stuck it into her rucksack. "So what the hell are we going to do all day? I can't stay cooped up inside these ugly cement walls. I'm way too antsy."

"Probably be a good idea to take a long nap before midnight."

"I can't sleep. I'm wound waay too tight for that."

"The mountain's still back there," he said. "Go commune with your mountain spirits."

She grinned and gave him a thumbs-up. She removed her sneakers and put on her hiking boots. "Wanna come along?" she asked.

"No thanks. I should conserve my energy. I'm feeling a little light-headed from my fast."

"You still trying to be like some kind of whacked-out holy dude or something, what with the fasting and celibacy?"

"No. I just feel I should be…pure. Unpolluted."

"Oh, so you think sex is dirty?"

"No. I think it must be wonderful. And when the time comes, I won't hold back."

"Boy, I hope I'm around for that. You'll go off like a gigantic Fourth of July fireworks show. Boom! Bam! KaBoom! Whoosh!" She fluttered her fingers dramatically in the air.

Kidd grinned through a bright blush. Rose's amusing crudity touched him deeply. Though he was agnostic, he said a silent prayer for her safety and well-being. He knew her guileless earthiness wouldn't be enough to keep her from getting lost in the Big Nowhere.

*   *   *

Just after noon he heard voices outside. Rita and Manuel were talking excitedly.

Kidd opened his door and stuck his head out.

Wearing tight jeans, boots and a brown leather jacket, Rita stood beside her Harley with a shiny black helmet dangling from her hand while Manuel did a little last-minute tinkering with the bike's mechanics. Kidd walked over to join them in front of the open bay of Manuel's garage.

"Hey, Kidd," Rita greeted. "I'm taking her out for a spin. Wanna come along?"

Kidd shook his head. "No thanks. I wouldn't want to spoil the moment."

"You should be honored," Manual told him. "First time the lovely Rita saddles up and rides in six years and you have a chance to ride along? How can you say no? This is history, man. In the making."

"What're you talking about, spoil the moment?" Rita asked Kidd. "I want to *share* the moment. And Manny here is afraid of motorcycles. You'd have to put a gun to his head to get him on one."

"That's right," said Manuel. "Them brain buckets won't do you no good when your head hits the highway."

Kidd equivocated. He looked at the bike, then looked at Rita, who was wearing the biggest smile he'd ever seen on her. "I don't know…"

"Come on, Kidd. You know you want to. I promise you you'll love it."

"Well…"

Rita said, "Get him my old helmet, will you, Manny?"

"*Sí, señora de jefe.* One brain-catcher coming up."

"He's kidding," Rita said. "He knows I'm a safe driver."

"Okay," said Kidd. He took a tentative step toward the Lowrider. It was a no-frills bike with black leather upholstery and flaring chrome exhaust pipes. Fringed black saddlebags hung over the rear wheel. Kidd caught his reflection in a square of gleaming chrome below the seat.

Rita mounted the motorcycle and put on her crash helmet.

Manuel came back with an old scuffed helmet with a dark visor. "Here ya go, Captain America. *Vaya con Dios.*"

Kidd put the helmet on and then climbed on the bike behind Rita, settling his rump on what he thought of as the "jump seat," though he didn't know what it was called by those who knew bikes. Remembering his dream of riding behind Rita as a contemporary Lady Godiva, he gripped her denim-clad hips and imagined his hands slipping around and up to cover her breasts. Then Rita hit the starter and the engine snarled, then roared, and his racy fantasy was lost to the sudden thrill of forward-lurching motion as the Lowrider bore them away.

"Hang tight," Rita shouted. "I won't bite."

Once they were on the highway and Kidd saw that Rita was indeed expert in handling the bike, he began to relax and enjoy the ride. Though he was flying unprotected over the blacktop at high speed, he was confident that Rita could keep them upright and above disaster. The sure grip of tires on asphalt and the way Rita controlled the tilt and lean of the vehicle only increased his confidence in her abilities. She turned onto a little-traveled country road and sure-handily put the Lowrider through its paces, accelerating to 70 mph.

As they rounded a hairpin curve, Kidd thought he saw something—a low-running shadow—keeping pace, but a double take revealed it to be his own shadow. He chuckled to himself. The roar of the motor made his laugh inaudible.

Rita decelerated and unexpectedly brought the bike to a stop at the entrance of a narrow dirt road. Before he could ask why they'd stopped, she looked back over her shoulder and asked him if he wanted to learn to drive the bike.

"Me?" he asked, foolishly. "I…I don't even know how to drive a car."

"All the more reason you should let me teach you to drive this bad boy. It's not rocket science, brainiac. Once you get the hang of it, there's nothing to it. All that horsepower between your legs, at your command…you'll get off on it, I guarantee."

"Thanks anyway," he demurred. "I think I'll pass."

"Look at it this way," she said as she removed her helmet. "If anything goes wrong over there in Never-Never Land and you find yourself alone in a ride-or-die situation, what're you gonna do? Say, 'Aw shit, I wish I'd listened to Rita,' while the monsters are eating your ass? Or jump on the bike and ride out of danger?"

She had him there, no argument. All he could say was, "Okay, let's do it. But don't blame me if I wreck your ride."

"I won't let that happen, baby. You'll find I'm a very good teacher."

After a few false starts, Kidd found that he could handle the bike without crashing into the dirt. Thirty minutes later, he was riding up and down the dirt road with relative ease, grinning like the happiest of fools.

"You *are* a good teacher," he said after he finally shut off the engine and dismounted.

"I am," Rita said. "But you're a good student. A natural-born biker."

"I didn't know it would be so much fun."

She suddenly grabbed his shoulders and kissed him full on the lips. "Welcome to the club, Kidd. Now if you can manage to survive the initiation, you're home-free."

She gave him a wink and an enigmatic smile.

CHAPTER THIRTEEN

He studied his reflection in the bathroom mirror. He grimaced. He bared his teeth and growled. He pulled his long hair back and gathered it into a tail and moved back a step from the sink. With two fingers of his free hand he covered his drooping mustache. He grunted, released the handful of hair, and then took another pull on the straw stuck in his carton of grape Juicy Juice. He was already feeling the sugar rush from what he'd drunk moments earlier. With no solid food in his digestive system, the sugar hit him hard and fast.

Eyeing the mirror warily, he reached for the scissors and began to cut uneven swatches from his shoulder-length hair.

Mirrors still spooked him sometimes. As a mentally ill child he had seen many an ogre, troll or worse, looking out at him from the other side of household mirrors. His parents and his doctors often had to reassure him that the creatures he saw in mirrors were not real, but he'd never completely believed them. Just because *they* couldn't see them didn't mean the monsters weren't there, staring at him with fiercely haunting eyes from the terrifying world on the backside of the looking glass.

An animated gargoyle's face appeared over his shoulder in the mirror, bulge-eyed and mouth crazily agape.

"Holy fuck, dude! Are you nuts?" Rose was standing behind him in the bathroom doorway. He hadn't heard her come in the front door. "Why are you butchering your hair?"

He shrugged. "Just am."

"I hope to hell your wonder cure ain't wearing off."

"It's not. I'm not nuts. I'm just cutting my hair. People do it everyday."

He put down the scissors and picked up the electric hair trimmer—one of the few things he had taken from his childhood home.

"You're gonna buzzcut it?"

He nodded.

"Give 'em here. I'll do it." She took the electric clippers out of his hand and began to cut his hair close to the scalp. It fell in stringy clumps to the tile. When she was done with his head, he pointed at his mustache and she removed that too. Then he handed her his electric razor and she buzzed the stubble off his dome.

"My God, look at you," she said. "You're just a kid."

"Aren't we all," he said.

"But you're a baldheaded kid."

He got the broom and dustpan and swept up his hair, then dumped it in the trashcan.

"Rita taught me how to ride her bike," he said as he examined the cranial bumps and contours of his bare head in the mirror. "Solo."

"I'll bet that's not the only thing she'll teach you to ride. I wonder how she'll like your skinhead look. Probably should've kept the 'stache though, so she won't think she's robbing the cradle."

"That's your fantasy, not mine."

Rose laughed. "Don't kid yourself, Kidd. I can read you like a rock."

He finished off his juice and dropped the empty carton in the trashcan, on top of the loose pile of his discarded hair. With a last neutral look at his mirror self, he said, "I'm going to sack out and catch some Z's. You should too. It's gonna be a long night."

"Not me. I reckon I'll hang in the Hoot and wait for the Fluckers. You wanna use the dream stone?"

"No. I just want to rest. You're not going to be drinking, are you?"

"Nothing stronger than a Coke. I'm gonna have another bowl of Rita's chili so I'll be good and gassed up for the most excellent trip."

He sat on the edge of the bed and yawned. Rose came over and rubbed his naked head. "For luck," she said.

*   *   *

As a small child he had the recurring nightmare that a motorcycle was under his crib. He would wake up screaming and crying in terror, babbling gibberish about the motorcycle under his bed. His parents did their best to reassure him that there was no such thing beneath him, rightly pointing out that a motorcycle wouldn't even fit under there. Why a motorcycle should be such an object of terror, neither Kidd nor his parents ever understood. Eyes big with terror, he once cried out from the crib: "Dark as a motorcycle." Some time later it became a family joke—one Kidd himself eventually found amusing. Why say "Dark as midnight" or "Black as pitch" when "Dark as a motorcycle" topped the familial repertoire of darkness metaphors? The humor helped to fend off fear.

Just before he dozed off, he wished with a pang of sadness that his parents were still alive so he could tell them that today he had finally mastered the dreaded motorcycle. They would've had a good laugh at that, surely.

Then, without benefit of Rose's dream stone, he dreamt that he was alone on the seat of a roaring bike, flying out of control down a moonlit road, barreling headlong toward a jagged outcropping of rock. He couldn't remember how to stop the runaway machine or how to slow it down. It was as if the bike had a mind of its own and foremost in its mechanical mind was killing the pitiful human on its back. The handlebars were locked. He could either jump off the bike or crash into the looming wall of rock.

"Wake up, Kidd. It's time to go."

He leapt off the bed as if jumping off the back of a moving motorcycle and crashed to the floor on his shoulder.

"Dude, what the fuck?"

He looked up at his rescuer, Rose. "Bad dream," he muttered.

"Throw some water on your face and get your shit together," she said. "Everybody's waiting on you. It's time to go."

"Yeah, okay," he said, getting to his feet.

Time had come at last. Time to go to a place that should not exist.

A place certain to be as dark as a motorcycle.

CHAPTER FOURTEEN

There was something more than excitement in the air, something more than affrighted anticipation. Kidd couldn't put a name to it yet, but a certain aura of *something* hung over the ragtag team as they waited at the alleged threshold of the lost road for the appointed hour to come round.

The moon in the cloudless night sky was just minutes from being full. Its soft milky light painted the landscape with a ghostly hue seldom found on an artist's canvas. The Hummer was parked on the weedy slip of a shoulder, hazard lights flashing. Rita had parked her Harley behind the vehicle and was smoking a cigarette and talking to Rose through the Hummer's backseat window.

His back to the others, Kidd shivered as he pissed in the ditch on the side of the two-lane. A juice fast was a good way to rid the body of toxins, but the downside was that you had to relieve yourself often. A cool roadside breeze polished his shaved head and he shivered harder.

"Shake it more than once, you're playing with it," Rita said with a hoarse laugh.

"Where have I heard that before?" he said, zipping his jeans before turning to face his companions.

"Five minutes, people," George said and then cranked the Hummer's engine.

"Ten-four, Cap'n," said Rita. She slapped the side of the Hummer, dropped her smoke and stepped on it, then walked toward her bike, zipping up her leather jacket. She wore her .357 Magnum low on her right hip.

She straddled the bike and put on her helmet. "I was just funning you, Kidd," she said in a conspiratorial tone. "There's nothing wrong with a little Miss Fist friction now and then. You looked so serious, I was just trying to lighten you up a little."

He paused with his hand on the Hummer's door handle. "This *is* serious. I want you to be serious and careful. You have to be."

"Don't worry." There was that enigmatic wink again.

"You should ride out front," he told her. Then he said to George, "Rita should go first. If she's behind us a troc could pick her off and we wouldn't even know it." He didn't know why he hadn't thought of this before now. He expected George to argue that they should stick to the original plan, but the man surprised him and agreed that Kidd's idea was obviously a good one.

"Roger that," Rita said. "I'll lead the parade."

Rita started the bike and it came alive with a throaty roar.

"Three minutes!" George shouted over the noise of the engines.

"I'm ready already!" Rita yelled back with blatant irritation.

Kidd sat in the shotgun-seat and slammed the door. He fastened the seatbelt and glanced back at Mallory and Rose. Eyes glittering with giddy excitement, Rose gave him the finger, then stuck her tongue out. Mallory touched a finger to the brim of her high-riding cowboy hat and smiled. Kidd picked up his pistol from the floorboard and made sure the safety was on.

"All systems go," George said in his Mission-Control voice.

The color screen of the GPS showed their location on the electronic map. The video camera mounted on the dash was on Standby. The night-vision camcorder was nestled between George's thighs.

"I feel like an astronaut," George said with a nervous chuckle.

"I feel like an idiot," Rose chimed in.

"As long as you don't act like one, hon," said Mallory with a wink.

Kidd glanced out the window. A single wispy cloud crossed the face of the waxing moon.

"Two minutes," said George.

Rita rode past the Hummer and stopped about ten yards ahead of it. She looked back and gave them a thumbs-up.

"A short ride for man," George said, "a fantastic journey for mankind."

"Dude, please..." Rose said.

"He'll be *so* disappointed if nothing happens," Mallory soberly observed.

"Oh, something will happen all right, Mal," said George. "I can feel it. Can't you, Kidd?"

"Yeah, maybe." Kidd felt that mysterious *something* again, and still he wasn't sure what it was.

"One minute!" shouted George. He clicked the dash cam to Record.

They spent the final sixty seconds in conversational silence. The guttural rumbling of motors spoke as one rough voice to the night. Then Kidd thought he finally understood the aura hanging about them like a diffuse halo, ominous beneath a bright harvest moon. It was the aura of the fated, enveloping everything in the inescapable blush of destiny.

And then the moon was officially full and they went roaring down the road, into the shimmering throat of the night.

*   *   *

"Come on…come on…*take* us," George said as if he were praying to a grudging god, beseeching the deity for admission to heaven.

Kidd glanced at the speedometer and saw that they were going sixty miles per hour. The compass had already gone haywire as it had on their practice run. The GPS monitor seemed to be working properly, giving their location as a red blip on the screen. The dash camera was digitally recording everything within the reach of the Hummer's headlight beams. Rita was ten or so yards in front of them, cutting a fine figure on her bike. In the pale wash of the headlights, her dark form suggested to Kidd a mythological Valkyrie, a priestess in black armor, riding on the back of a monstrous wolf, seeking the souls of fallen heroes for the purpose of conducting them to Odin's great hall in Valhalla.

All the Hummer's windows were wide open to the night and cold air washed in erratic waves over the passengers. Kidd's leather bomber jacket kept the cold from biting too deep. Rose's fatigue jacket apparently wasn't keeping her warm enough because she shouted, "I'm freezing my tits off back here!" Mallory in her Western-style denim jacket and cowboy hat made no complaint. George looked snug in his fur-collared sheepherder jacket and was probably too preoccupied with his prayerlike prods to notice the cold anyway.

"Come on…"

"Jeezus I'm freezing."

"It's not going to happen," Mallory suddenly lamented.

"Yes it is," George shot back. "Come *on*…"

Kidd scanned both sides of the road for signs of troc activity. He saw nothing out of the ordinary. Aside from the compass going crazy, everything seemed monotonously normal. He was beginning to think that Mallory was right when she said it wasn't going to happen. He was both let down and relieved at the prospect of their night ride going bust, most of his relief centering on Rita, who was most exposed to potential danger.

"Uh-oh," Rose said. "Check out the GPS doohickey."

Kidd looked. The red blip denoting their position on the map was flashing, fading in and out. Then an "Error" message appeared in the middle of the screen, followed by a boxed message: "No signal."

"It can't find the satellites," George said. "By God, I think we're going!"

"Fuck that, I think we're already gone," Rose said. "I feel weird. And that sound! You hear what I hear?"

Kidd hadn't noticed it until now, and now that he did, he realized that the sound had been building in volume and intensity for several minutes, masked by the rush of wind and rumble of engines. It was a low-pitched hum, similar to a sustained bass note on a pipe organ. It had started as a single note but now other notes were joining in to make a deeply cavernous chord, swelling dramatically, thrumming up from the road and the surrounding nightscape.

"I hear it now," Mallory said with anxiety in her voice.

"Did this happen last time?" Kidd asked. "This noise?"

"No, nothing like this," George said with a grin that could've just as easily been a grimace.

"It *hurts*," Mallory said with a shrill note of uncharacteristic hysteria.

"Roll the damn windows up!" shouted Rose.

Kidd touched the scar under his eye. Had it twitched? His fingertip explored the fibrous tissue like a blind man reading Braille, but it told him nothing. He peered through the windshield and locked his eyes on Rita, who was maintaining a steady ten-yard lead.

The humming sound continued to increase in volume, building, no doubt, to an inevitable crescendo.

Up ahead, beyond the reach of the Harley's single headlamp, something was charging relentlessly toward them. Kidd felt it coming, though he wasn't sure what it was. They were *going* and it was *coming*, and the impending collision of forces took his breath away. He braced for the impact, eyes still fixed on Rita's back.

"Oh Jesus," Mallory moaned.

Then it hit them.

A visible shock wave that looked like a transparent tunnel pulsing with enormous energy, a hardening corridor that looked as if it might've just now been created by a godlike glassblower, and they were riding right into it—right down its gullet.

Rose yelped.

Rita's bike wobbled and would've gone down had she not been such a skilled rider.

George cursed as he bolted upright and desperately tightened his grip on the steering wheel, fighting for control of the vehicle.

Then came the booming crescendo and a blinding flash of light. The world tilted on a skewed axis, and Kidd instinctively knew they had breached the barrier to another world.

CHAPTER FIFTEEN

The world seemed to right itself in the next instant, but Kidd had no confidence that anything in this strange place would *stay* righted.

"Holy Mary, Mother of God." This from George, who doubtlessly thought they needed a benediction.

Rita veered her bike to the right and quickly dropped speed. The Hummer blew past her.

"Stop," Kidd said. "Now!"

George obeyed Kidd's command. A moment later the Hummer lurched to a halt in the middle of the road. Kidd stuck his head out the window and looked back. Rita had stopped on the side of the road, her foot on the ground to balance the bike and keep it upright. She saw him looking and made a circular motion with her hand in the air. Then she pushed off, rode up and stopped beside the Hummer.

"Holy crap, Kidd, y'all were right," she said. She glanced around at the moonlit surroundings. "Where the hell *are* we?"

"We're *here*," said George, his face captive to an idiotic grin. He turned off the Hummer's engine.

"Here being…?" Rita cut her engine.

"The Big Nowhere," Rose offered.

Anxious that Rita was so vulnerable on the back of her bike, Kidd threw open his door, stepped out with the gun in his fist and scanned the surrounding landscape.

"The Land of Oz," Mallory said.

"Follow the spooky black road," Rose said in nervous Munchkin singsong.

"Listen!" George urged his companions.

No one spoke for a long moment.

"It's so quiet," said George.

"*Too quiet,*" Rose said with a brittle laugh.

Kidd took in the uneven lay of the moonlit land. Where before there had been trees, grass and sporadic signs of civilization, now there was only a broken landscape of craggy rocks with no vegetation at all. The road itself was different; rather than appearing manmade, it looked organic, as if the ground had grown it, as if it were a dark vein in the stony flesh of an immense creature whose back they now found themselves on. There were numerous fissures in the road's surface, some as much as six inches in width.

He looked up at the full moon. It appeared to be slightly larger than it was back in the familiar territory of their home world, but maybe the clearer atmosphere just made it seem so. A surprising number of stars were crisply visible, refusing to be outshone by the ripe moon.

A sharp metallic snap and a dull clunk broke the long silence as George Flucker opened his door and got out of the vehicle with the short flagpole and furled stars and stripes in his hand.

"Good luck getting that in this ground," Rita told him.

"Be careful, hon," Mallory told him.

"Let your freak flag fly," Rose told him.

Kidd told him nothing. He was back to scanning the landscape for dangerous predators.

Mallory opened her door and got out with the night-vision video camera in her hand. George was looking for a suitable place to plant the flagpole. Mallory brought the camera to her eye and began to record him.

Rose likewise got out of the vehicle. "I feel woozy," she said. "Like I just got off a monster Six Flags ride."

"That was way better than Six Flags," said Rita, still in the saddle. "Like riding lightning."

"I hope we can ride out of here as easy as we rode in," said Kidd, satisfied for the moment that there were no trocs around.

"It's all rock," George said. "No loose dirt that I can see. Ah, here's a place I can wedge the pole."

Then he turned to his wife and said, "You getting this?" He unfurled the flag and secured the flagpole in a small pocket between darkly veined rocks. "I claim this land in the name of the United States of America. Long may she wave."

"Stars and stripes forever," Mallory said from behind the camera.

"I don't know, man," Rose said as she bent down with her rock hammer in her hand. "This land here looks badass enough to claim *us*."

George posed for the video, one hand resting on the flagpole. He beamed a big smile. Mallory moved in for a close-up.

Rose began to tap the edge of the black road with her hammer. *Tink, tink tink.* She chipped off several small pieces and dropped them into a glassine bag. "Igneous," she said, all business now, "but not like any I've seen before. Flecks of something else in it I can't identify. Not in this fucking light."

"George?" Mallory said, something strange in her voice. "*George.*"

"What is it, hon?" George asked.

She was still looking through the viewfinder but she had shifted her aim off her husband and was looking down the road.

"I think there's a car down there."

*   *   *

"It's an SUV," George said when he looked through the night-vision video camera. "A Ford, looks like."

"I'll ride down and take a look," Rita said.

"We better stay together," George said. "We'll all go. Everybody, back in the vehicle. Chop-chop."

"Chop-chop my ass," muttered Rose. "You're not the boss of me."

"You want to stay here by yourself?" Mallory asked her.

Rose didn't answer. She wished everybody would just shut up long enough for her to hear what the rocky ground was saying to her. It had started whispering to her after she'd chipped off samples from this weird road. The rocks were trying to tell her something, something important. She knew she wasn't hallucinating. She could almost always tell when she was hallucinating, and she knew she wasn't, not now. The rocks were talking to her but she didn't know yet what they were saying because people kept running their fucking mouths. The land spoke in murmuring whispers, a chorus of windy fricatives, insistent and demanding.

Then the motorcycle roared to life and the voices were lost to its ugly blatting rumble that made her think of a hulking monster's fart that just wouldn't quit.

Rose gave up for the time being, and got back in the Hummer.

She didn't tell the others what she'd heard—*almost* heard. If she did, they would think she'd gone for a quick dip in the crazy pool. She didn't want to put herself in the position of defending her sanity, especially not to that pompous asshole George Flucker. (Well, maybe not an outright asshole but shamefully high on his own fumes, for sure.) She would wait until she was able to decipher the message and *then* tell them what it said—if she thought they needed to hear it.

You're not the boss of me. What a childish thing to say! She would have to choose her words more carefully now. She wasn't in the habit of censoring her comments, but she needed these people to take her seriously. Their lives might depend on it. Hers too. She was not going to let them discount what she might say as the words of a foul-mouthed nutcase, a crazy rock-hunting kid. She was twenty-four years old and if there was one thing she knew, it was how to read rocks. And these rocks—and the very ground itself—were trying to tell her something terribly important.

Trouble was, Rose liked to shock people. Her grandfather had christened her his "little firecracker" and she had always done her best to live up to that name, her fuse always alight and crackling toward little explosions of jarring irreverence or outright vulgarities. Okay, she would rein herself in a bit so these good folks would take her more seriously. She would choose her words with a little more care and bite her frigging tongue if she had to. And if that didn't work, screw 'em. She wasn't going to be a tight-ass phony for any whitebread bozo that couldn't accept her for what she was.

She stared at the back of Kidd's shorn head (she wasn't sold on his Gandhi look) as George started them down the road toward the SUV.

She said, "Kidd, you know the dream stone?"

He turned half around to give her a puzzled look and said, "Yeah?"

"Well, these monster rocks here have a lot to say," she said, "but I couldn't get the message for all the noise."

Kidd shrugged and went eyes-front again. He was on the lookout for trocs and obviously didn't want to be distracted. That was okay. She felt better now that she'd at least told somebody about the attempted communication. She knew that sooner or later she would get the message.

"I hope you're here, Brother Owl," she whispered.

*   *   *

The Hummer bumped along the road at 30 miles per hour toward the SUV, which was now about thirty yards ahead of them. Rita this time was riding alongside the Hummer.

Kidd kept his eyes locked on the SUV. In his dream-stone dream there had been dozens of abandoned autos, some containing the skeletal remains of former passengers. The closer they got to the vehicle, the faster his heart thumped. He wasn't sure he wanted to see what was inside the SUV. He briefly wondered what Rose meant when she said these monster rocks have a lot to say. Was she speaking strictly geologically or did she mean they were actually trying to talk to her?

"That's a Georgia tag," George said as the Ford's license plate shone with a reflective glow. "Kidd, can you make out the county and the year?"

"No, but in another minute we'll be right on top of it and you can see for yourself."

With a nervous laugh, George said, "Guess I'm a bit impatient."

"Should we be this far from where we came in?" asked Mallory, leaning forward again. "We don't want to lose sight of the way out."

"We're fine," said George. "Relax, hon."

"I don't mind telling you, I'm shaking in my boots," she said.

"Nice boots, by the way," Rose said. "Wild West shitkickers for sure. Matches the hat."

"Yeah, thanks."

The Hummer stopped smoothly, immediately behind the Ford SUV. The driver's door of the Ford was open. Rita stopped abreast of the dusty blue vehicle. The expiration date on the license plate was Aug 2003, the county of residence was Toombs.

"A long way from home," George said. "Toombs, I mean."

"That's down Vidalia way," said Mallory. "We went to the Onion Festival a couple of years ago."

"I'll bet that was a hoot and a half," said Rose. "Imagine being Onion Queen. After that, the rest of your life would be a big-ass letdown."

"Ladies, wait in the car. Kidd, there's a flashlight in the glove box. Ready?"

"Yeah," Kidd said when the flashlight was in his hand.

"Let's go." George got out and immediately started shooting the rear of the SUV with the night-vision video camera.

Kidd went straight to the open driver's door of the derelict auto and shone the light inside.

Rita had dismounted and came to stand beside him. "Bloodstains on the seat," she said.

"And on the inside of the door," he pointed out. "Key still in the ignition, still turned on but the battery's long dead."

"Stand aside," said George, "so I can shoot the interior. Kidd, go to the other side and see if the registration is in the glove box."

Rita stood back and Kidd went around to the other side of the vehicle. The passenger door opened with a rusty groan. He stuck his pistol in the waist of his jeans and rifled the glove box's clutter of CDs, fast-food napkins and a small Star Wars toy until he found the vehicle's registration. He read aloud for the video. "John Monroe Single, 354 Pinewood Circle, Baxley, Georgia. Born 1963."

"Taken in 1998," George said. "If his registration was up to date."

"Taken and slaughtered," Rita added, "judging by the amount of blood he lost."

Kidd returned the registration to the glove box and snicked it shut. He touched his scar and said, "His bones are probably out there in the rocks, unless they have some use for them."

"Like what?" she asked.

"I don't know. Maybe they take trophies or make crude tools. Or maybe they're strictly hunters."

"Yeah, well, I think we've been here long enough," she opined. "You found your stolen road, you planted the flag and tagged a missing car and driver, so let's get the hell out of here before some of those monsters show up for a midnight snack."

Kidd scarcely heard her. He was staring off at the rock-ridged landscape on the left side of the road. He walked to the road's edge and shone his light at the place where the land dropped off into a crevasse.

"What is it, Kidd?" George asked.

"Sweet Jesus," Rita said when she saw what was at the end of Kidd's shaky flashlight beam.

CHAPTER SIXTEEN

"What are they looking at?" Mallory asked, squirming in the Hummer's backseat.

"Damned if I know," Rose said. "Let's get out of this deathtrap and find out."

"Deathtrap? Why do you call it that? This isn't a deathtrap. It's one of the safest—"

Rose threw open her door and slid off the seat. Why *had* she called it a deathtrap? Had she picked up some sort of subliminal message from the whispering rocks? A precognitive warning? She couldn't be sure, but it seemed damned prudent to get the hell out and see what the others were looking at so intently. "Come on, Tex," she said to Mallory. "Them boots are made for walking."

Mallory slid out after her and put her boots on the ground. "I loved that song when I was little," she said. "My mother played it all the time. She *loved* Nancy Sinatra. Never cared for her daddy though. Him and his mob pals."

Realizing that Mallory babbled when she was scared and that she was babbling scared right now, Rose started toward the side of the road where Kidd, Rita and George were huddled with their backs to her, peering over the rocky precipice.

"I wish you wouldn't call me Tex," Mallory said. "I'm not from Texas. I'm from Arizona."

"Shake a tail feather, Arizona. There's something really weird over there."

Mallory caught up with her. "Holy crow! Is that...?"

"A truckload of dead babies," Rose said with a catch in her voice. She felt as if her heart had jumped into her throat for a tête-à-tête with her tonsils.

Down there in the jagged rocks was a big rig with a broken back, its dented silver trailer lying on its side, rear door hanging open. Scattered over the treacherous ground were dozens of little blond-haired corpses in identical red dresses. Some of them were in tiny lidless coffins.

"Dolls," Mallory said. "Baby dolls, hon. Not dead babies."

"I hate dolls," Rose said. "They creep me out."

"Those look like Baby Beverlys. They were real popular a few years back."

Rose saw that they *were* dolls and that the coffins were cardboard boxes. She screwed her eyes shut, then opened them again to watch Kidd play his light beam over the scattered dolls and the wrecked rig. The jagged rock ridges looked like rows and rows of brown teeth. Standing on the road was like being in the open mouth of a colossal beast, waiting for the teeth to tear you to shreds and for the colossus to swallow you down.

George was shooting video of the wreckage.

Hands on her slim hips, Rita said, "Don't do it, Kidd. It's too dangerous."

"Don't do what?" Rose asked.

"He wants to climb down there and check the cab of the truck," Rita said.

"I'll be fine," said Kidd.

"I'm going too," Rose told him. "I want a closer look at those bitchin' rock formations. And some samples to take back."

"No, Rose," Mallory said. "You don't—"

"Hey, I'm a rockhound, remember? And a helluva rock climber. If my idiot blood bro is going, so am I."

Kidd gave her a look of concern, mirroring Rita's expression.

Rose slapped his shoulder. "How 'bout it, bro? You ready to rock'n'roll into those rocks?"

*   *   *

Kidd nodded. The big brother part of him didn't want Rose to go down there with him. She was the boyish kid sister, too reckless by half in the way she did things, small-boned and vulnerable, too trusting of the ways of the world—or in this case, the otherworld. Yet he knew she was an experienced rock climber and that her small stature made her a much better climber than he was. She would be in her element down there among those tooth-like stony protrusions, as sure-footed as a lizard.

But there might be trocs hiding in the rocks and moon shadows. And no human was lizard-footed enough to outrun or out-maneuver a troc. Not here on their home turf.

She adjusted the strap of her canvas shoulder bag so that the bag rested against her left buttock, then she turned her ballcap backwards and grinned. "Follow my lead, Kidd-o," she said. "It'll be a breeze."

"This should make for some great footage," said George, tapping a forefinger against the camera.

"Be careful, kids," Mallory said.

Rita unholstered her pistol and said, "I got your back."

Rose started down the steep incline and Kidd followed.

The video made him self-conscious but the climb down required such great concentration that he quickly forgot all about the camera at his back.

*   *   *

Bad juju. That's what Rita's old biker buddy Johnny Headstone would've said of this strange road and its environs. Then right on cue: *This place reeks of bad juju,* Headstone whispered in her head. *Big-time badass vibes, Legs.* That was his nickname for her because of her long legs. Johnny had been a fearless wheeling daredevil on a bike—until he dared the devil one time too many. Then the fastest wheels he drove were on his wheelchair, paralyzed as he was, below the waist. He's eaten his gun less than a year later.

Bad road, Legs baby, and the juju ain't good.

"I hear ya," Rita whispered back.

"What's that, hon?" asked Mallory.

"Nothing. Just talking to myself."

"Sometimes a gal has to be her own best company."

"It's not that. You're all fine company. It's this place. It's...not a good place to be."

"Oh, I know. I'm so scared I'm about to wet my britches. But we won't be here much longer." Mallory glanced at her wristwatch. "We won't be here more than an hour. George is very strict on that point."

For his part, George was oblivious to their conversation, so intent was he on shooting video of Kidd and Rose, who were now less than a hundred feet from the wreckage, and closing.

Rita kept her eyes on them as they scaled low hurdles of outcropped rock. The moon was so bright she had little difficulty in following their progress. Kidd was struggling to keep up with Rose, the more experienced climber. When Rose disappeared behind a particularly high uneven wall of stone, Rita stepped off the edge of the road, ready to go down there after her, but then Rose came out of eclipse at the perimeter of the doll-strewn wreckage, and Rita relaxed a little.

"All this time everybody thought the Twilight Zone was only an old TV show," Mallory was saying, "but here we are, smack dab in the middle of it."

Put this shit in your rearview, Legs, whispered Johnny Headstone, *ride out while you can.*

*   *   *

Rose nudged a doll with the toe of her hiking boot, then bent down and picked it up. Its eyes opened and she dropped it before it could take a bite out of her. "Fugly little bitch," she said. "I fucking hate dolls. The way they look at me. My momma gave me one of those Cabbage Patch brats when I was little and I tried to flush it down the john."

Winded from the physical exertion, Kidd made a chuffing sound that was probably meant to be laughter.

"These ones are worse," she said, kicking one of them in its little rubberized head. "Baby Beverly, my ass. Baby Beelzebub's more like it."

Kidd pulled the flashlight from his hip pocket and aimed it at the rectangle of yawning blackness at the open end of the silver semi.

"What? You see something in there?" Rose asked.

"No, I'm just making sure nothing's hiding in there."

The flashlight beam played over unopened brown boxes of Baby Beverly dolls.

"No creepy critters," said Rose. "What happened here? You think the trocs ran him off the road?"

"Hard to imagine, a big rig like this. Let's check out the cab."

They made their way to the tractor, which was upright, though leaning against a ridge of jagged rock with its left wheels off the ground. The door to the cab was shut. Kidd climbed up on the small metal platform below the door, gripped the handle, pulled hard and the door came open with a loud creak. He shone the light inside.

"There a dead guy in there?" Rose asked.

"No. Nothing. No bloodstains this time."

"Maybe he got away."

"Where would he go?"

"I dunno. Maybe he ran back up the road and back to the world."

Kidd slid into the seat on his knees and shone the light in the sleeper compartment behind the seat. There was a double-decker bunk built into the upholstered wall. Lying on the neatly made lower bunk with his head on the pillow was a Teddy bear. Immediately behind the driver's seat there was a compact desk with a storage bin above it. Kidd had seen the interior of a lot of trucks while hitchhiking, and this was a nicer one with economic use of available space. A man could live comfortably here indefinitely—if he had an unlimited supply of food and water.

"Whadda you see?' asked Rose.

On the desktop: a spiral notebook, a SpongeBob SquarePants coloring book and a box of crayons. On top of the notebook was a man's wallet.

"Bro? What is it?"

Kidd cleared his throat and said, "I think the driver had his kid with him." He opened the wallet and the owner's driver's license fell out. Florida license issued to Donald James McKay, age 39. The man in the photo was tanned and his expression was affable. He looked like a guy you might enjoy a beer with. In the wallet was a photo of a cute little girl, maybe 5 years old, with long light-brown hair and impish smile.

"Looks like he left this here in case anybody came along to find it," he said.

"Great," Rose said. "If we ever get our asses out of here we can report it to...whoever the fuck you report shit like this to. Let's get out of here while the getting is good. If it is."

CHAPTER SEVENTEEN

George Flucker was growing impatient. The footage he was getting with the night-vision video camera was not all that striking or dramatic. In fact, there was nothing in the viewfinder to prove that it was being shot in another—starker—reality. For all intents and purposes, this might've been wreckage filmed at a mundane site in Colorado or New Mexico. A tractor-trailer had run off the road and crashed onto the rocks, spilling its cargo of dolls. So *what?* What he needed was a video record of something extraordinary. What he wanted was video of one of those creatures Kidd called trocs. Moreover, what he truly wanted was a dead creature to take back with them as undeniable and dramatic proof of the existence of an unknown predatory life form. Such physical evidence surely would make the world take the report of this excursion seriously. Coupled with whatever video evidence the dash cam had captured when they crossed over, the workaday world would be obliged to stand up and take very close notice.

"They're taking too long," Rita said. Then she cupped a hand round the corner of her mouth and shouted: "Hurry up down there!"

It was then that George saw something move at the left edge of the viewfinder's ghostly green image. Kidd had just jumped down from the cab of the truck with what looked like a spiral notebook in his hand, and Rose was bending down with her hammer to chip off a sample from an ankle-high edge of a rock. George moved the camera a little to the left and centered the shot on a green-tinted shadow that seemed to be crouching now behind a chest-high protrusion of rock no more than five or six yards from Rose.

George zoomed in on the shadow, which was no longer moving. Was it more than an innocent shadow? Had his uneasy imagination created a crouching creature out of whole-cloth darkness?

Then the shadow's eyes caught the moonlight and glowed with demonic fire.

*   *   *

"Look out! On your right! Shoot it!"

George's urgent shouts froze Kidd to the spot on which he was standing. Then he glanced to his right, forgetting for the moment that he had a flashlight in his hand. As it turned out, he didn't need a flashlight to see the thing crouched and only half-hidden by a low wall of rock that resembled a row of broken teeth.

Kidd tried to pull his pistol but its hammer caught on his belt and the gun remained in his pants. He twisted it and yanked it free, but the troc was already coming over that dental wall of rocks, flying in a powerful leap at Rose.

Rose had come out of her bent-over posture and now raised her hammer in a futile gesture of defense as the creature flew at her.

*   *   *

Rita didn't need a night scope to see the monster. The full moon gave her all the light she needed to catch the beast in her gunsight. From her elevated angle, the trajectory of the troc's leap was a short arc, giving her a decent shot at the moving target. A less experienced shooter likely would've fired behind the thing and missed, but Rita's reflexes were acute, her shooter's instinct unfailing. She fired a double-tap. *Pop-pop!*

The troc's torso twitched and twisted in flight, and the creature crashed headfirst to the ground at Rose's feet. It thrashed violently against the rocky ground. Rose bent over and slammed her hammer against the troc's skull and it stopped thrashing.

"Thank you, Jesus," Mallory said.

"Thank you, Smith & Wesson," said Rita.

"I got it!" George gleefully yelled. "By God, I recorded it all."

Down below, Rose called out: "Holy shit, look at this ugly fucker!"

*   *   *

Rita hurried back from the Hummer with the rifle in her hands. She passed George, who was carrying the folded body bag he'd retrieved from the vehicle. "You can get almost anything from Amazon," he'd explained before she had a chance to ask.

Mallory had temporarily taken over video duties and stood ready on the road's edge to record any further action. Kidd and Rose were still standing over the dead troc, Kidd with the flashlight in one hand and the pistol in the other, apparently ready to put more lead in it if the thing showed signs of life.

George hurled the body bag down to them and said, "See if you can fit it in the bag and drag it up here."

"I'm not touching that thing," Rose announced.

"I'll do it," Kidd said, his voice a soft echo against the rocky terrain.

Rita stood at the edge of the road with the .30-06 cradled in her arms, keeping her eyes peeled for more monsters.

Mallory said loud enough for everyone to hear: "We've been here twenty-five minutes. Don't dawdle. Time's getting short." Then she added, "We don't want to get stuck over here."

Keep your shit tight, Legs, there's more of 'em out there in the shadows, Johnny Headstone whispered from his haunted wheelchair somewhere back in the real world. When Rita had first joined the Rebel Riders, Johnny Headstone had taken her under his muscular wing and protected her from cretins like Fathead Frank, who wanted to make her his "bitch." Johnny had coldcocked Fathead and made it clear to the rest of the gang that "Legs ain't nobody's bitch. She's a Rider, same as the rest of you sonsabitches, but a helluva a lot prettier." Fathead, being as thick-headed as his nickname suggested, was slow in getting the message and Johnny was obliged to pound the point home with his fists on two subsequent occasions, making an example of Fathead by permanently altering the skew of his bulbous nose and adding an exclamation mark in the shape of a slanted scar on his upper lip. Later, when Rita won the Ride & Shoot trophy, Johnny Headstone beamed like a proud big brother and roared: "I told you assholes she was a

Rider, a better man than the lot of you."

Rita watched the moon-shadowed rocks while Kidd unrolled the body bag beside the dead creature. She clicked off the rifle's safety and waited for a new target to present itself.

*   *   *

"It's too big for the bag," said Rose, who now held the flashlight.

"Not if I bend his legs," Kidd said.

"How do you know it's a he? I don't see a dick."

"I don't." He unzipped the bag, spread it open and rolled the monstrous corpse into it.

"Don't see a pussy either," Rose said. "How the hell do these fuckers reproduce?"

"Stop looking for sex organs and watch out for this thing's buddies."

"I'm watching. Give me the gun."

He pulled it from his belt and handed it to her. Then he went back to trying to fit the beast into the bag. This was the first time he'd been this close to a troc since the night of the fatal auto accident, the night of his scarring. If his memory served him well, this dead one was quite a bit bigger than the one that had been midwife to his dad's passing—the one that had marked Kidd for life with its long talon before disappearing into the storm-ridden night. This one had part of its skull blown away by Rita's .357 Magnum, and a bullet hole in the center of its chest. Reddish-orange blood seeped from both wounds and seemed to glow in the moonlight.

He tried to bend the creature's long legs at the knees but those lower appendages were stiff and unyielding. He tried bending them one at a time, putting more elbow grease into the effort, and finally the first one bent to Kidd's will and he managed to slip the leathery leg into the bag.

As he set to work on the other leg, he wondered why his scar hadn't alerted him to this troc's presence before it showed itself in attack. Did the scar only work as troc-detector back in the civilized world? That ability apparently was of no use here. Here, anyone could see them.

Evidently, the same principle applied to the scar. Here in Troc Land, Kidd had no special abilities, or so it seemed.

What if it works in reverse here? What if the scar somehow alerts the trocs to my presence and draws them like blood in the water draws sharks? No, he had no reason to think this was the case. It was nothing more than a preposterous notion feeding off his fear.

The second leg went into the bag and Kidd dropped back on his haunches to catch his breath.

"Hurry up, dude," Rose said. "Our asses are hanging out in the breeze like tasty bait."

"Twenty minutes to go!" Mallory the timekeeper shouted.

Kidd leaned forward and tried to zip the bag shut but zipper couldn't close its metal teeth over the troc's bent legs. "Give me your hammer," he said to Rose.

"What?" She put the flashlight beam in his face.

"Give me your hammer. And don't shine that in my face."

She gave him the rock hammer and said, "Oh, I get it. Good thinking, bro."

Kidd raised the hammer and brought it down with both hands on the creature's left leg. Inside the pebbled skin, the thin bone snapped with the sound of a small firecracker exploding inside a paper bag.

"Take that, you fugly ucker," Rose said to the dead troc.

Kidd hammered the right leg, but this time there was no rewarding pop. He struck it again. And again. The third strike broke the bone, and Kidd zipped the body bag shut.

Kidd stuck the hammer in his belt, then reached back to make sure the spiral notebook he'd found in the truck was still rolled up and secure in his hip pocket. It was. "Okay," he said, "let's get the hell out of here. Help me get it onto my shoulder."

It took several attempts, but he and Rose finally managed to get the bagged troc onto Kidd's shoulder in a modified fireman's carry.

"God, this thing stinks," Rose observed, wrinkling her nose and backing away from Kidd and the thing he carried.

With the truck and the scatter of dolls at their backs, and with the wind picking up speed as it moaned over the rocks, they were just beginning to make their way over the ridges of rock and back toward the road above them when a rifle-shot cracked the uneasy silence and someone yelled: "Behind you! Another one!"

*　　*　　*

Rita saw it coming out of the shadows, raised the rifle to her shoulder and fired just as it leapt off the ground. Knocked off course, the beast took a header into an upthrust edge of rock and lay still in an ungainly sprawl. Another troc reared its head behind a low wall. Rita zeroed on it and fired. The top of the thing's head exploded.

"They're everywhere!" George shouted.

And they were. The rocks were crawling with the creatures. Thankfully, Rita had sufficient light from the remarkably bright full moon to pick her targets and shoot true. She had felled four of them by the time George put down the camera and started firing his pistol.

But there were too many of them. There was a small army of trocs down there and they were closing in from every direction on Rose and Kidd.

"The truck!" shouted Mallory. "Run for the truck!"

Rose turned toward the wrecked truck and shot down one of the beasts blocking their way to the safety of the truck's cab. Another one charged at her and she put it down with a well-placed headshot. Then she and Kidd were running toward the truck, leaving the body-bagged troc behind.

Rita saw a smaller one dogging Kidd's heels but she couldn't shoot at it without putting him in the path of the bullet. But if she didn't shoot it, the monster would surely take Kidd down from behind.

"Shit!" she said as the troc bounded forward and took Kidd to the ground.

Rose had faced away from Kidd to fire at another advancing creature, so she was oblivious to his deadly plight.

Rita stood in a shooter's stance, finger on the trigger and cheek nearly touching the rifle's stock as if she expected the weapon to whisper something vital in her ear. She kept Kidd's attacker in her sights but she could not bring herself to risk the shot.

*   *   *

Kidd hit the ground face-first. His front teeth broke against a rock shelf and blood gushed from his split lips as the troc's talons ripped through his bomber jacket and sank into the flesh of his upper back. The creature's teeth snapped at his neck, nicking his skin.

He had managed to pull the rock hammer from his belt, but the troc was fastened to his back like a tenacious leech and the best Kidd could do was hammer blindly over his right shoulder at the monster's head. With a necessarily short stroke, he swung the hammer and struck a glancing blow to the troc's skull. If it wasn't enough to do much damage, the blow at least forestalled an immediate follow-up attack of the creature's jaws on the back of Kidd's neck.

He swung again and succeeded only in smashing the hammer's head against his own scapula. With a grunt of pain and frustration, he adjusted his blind aim and swung again, this time hitting, he presumed, the troc's shoulder.

He smelled the creature's fishy breath and felt its clamminess on his neck.

Even as he twisted and jerked his shoulders in a final attempt to free himself from the troc's stubborn piercing grasp, Kidd could feel the deathblow coming before it actually struck, and he knew the monster's powerful jaws were going to crunch the vertebrae of his neck and sever his head in a single killing snap.

CHAPTER EIGHTEEN

Rose dispatched another troc to Big Nowhere hell, then turned to see the beast grappling on Kidd's back. She all at once felt as if she were a passive member of a movie audience, about to witness a gruesome display of theatrical violence. Her impulse was to hide her eyes and turn away to avoid seeing a bloody scene certain to give her nightmares long into the future.

Then she remembered that she too was an actor in this drama, not on a silver screen but on this bizarre open-air stage. Her leading man was seconds away from death—*real* death, not that "Now I die" Shakespearean crapola.

She stepped close to the beast, jammed the muzzle against the side of its head and fired. The thing reared up as if it were going to let loose with a howl, then it stiffened, shivered convulsively and collapsed on Kidd's back with a wheezing glissando that reminded her of a vacuum cleaner shutting down.

Though she hated the thought of touching the dead monster, she bent down and tried to push it off Kidd's back. The thing was heavier than it looked, but she succeeded in rolling it off him.

"You all right?" she asked him as she squatted beside him and placed a hand on his shoulder.

Kidd got to his feet, his eyes darting about to spot any new attacker. "Think so."

Rose could tell by his bewildered expression, his bloodied mouth and his crazy eyes that Kidd's close encounter with the troc had stunned him and left him disoriented. She seized the sleeve of his jacket, turned him toward the tractor-trailer and said, "Run for the truck."

There was a trio of fierce trocs between them and the haven of the truck's cab. Rose felt as if she and Kidd were caught up in a psychotic game of Red Rover, playing against a team of brutal aliens from a tougher neighborhood in the galaxy. If you won, you got to live. You didn't let yourself think about losing. You just ran for shelter, shooting on the run and praying that Rita's shooting would be worthy of a Troc Shoot trophy.

A slug ricocheted off a rock and zinged past Rose's left ear. "Sonofabitch," she muttered, thinking that she just might make it to safety if George didn't accidentally kill her first.

*   *   *

Five or six trocs had broken off from their loose formation around Kidd and Rose and were charging up the incline toward the road where the shooters were methodically thinning the beasts' numbers. Rita ignored them and concentrated her fire on the trocs positioned to intercept Kidd and Rose. She hoped George would be smart enough to use his pistol on the ones scaling the rocky incline with murderous intentions. If he could slow their advance long enough for her to see her two friends to safety, then she could turn her firepower on the remaining chargers and cut them down before they could top the rocky incline and reach the road. The ugly buggers were *fast*. Nearly as quick as lizards. And they could leap as powerfully as lions, but with more quickness due to their lighter weight and streamlined shape.

Rita popped in a new ammo clip and then shot a troc off its crouching perch on top of the cab of the truck.

Kidd threw open the driver's door, handed Rose inside, then jumped in behind her and slammed the door just as a small troc leapt at him. The baby troc hit the door and fell backward. Rita shot it where it lay.

Then she turned her attention to the troc that was scampering up the incline toward her, its eyes locked on her as its claws clicked against rock. She shot it between its eyes and it slid to the bottom of the incline.

George had dropped two of the chargers before they got halfway up to the road, so now there were only two trocs scrabbling up the slope at them. Rita coolly killed them both with headshots.

One troc had climbed onto the hood of the truck and was pounding the windshield with its arm, eager to get at the occupants. Rita took aim and blew it off the truck.

The dozen or so remaining beasts retreated into the surrounding shadows and faded from sight. Rita lowered her weapon and looked around. Trouper that she was, Mallory continued to record the scene of carnage with the video camera. She'd picked it up again when George realized that shooting his gun was more vital than shooting video. George looked up from reloading his pistol and said, "That was amazing. Amazing!" Though she didn't quite know why, Rita wanted to slam the butt of the rifle into the man's face.

"I think I'm gonna be sick," Mallory said, letting the camera hang from her right hand. Then she bent over and vomited on the road.

*   *   *

Kidd touched his bleeding lips and delicately probed his upper front teeth with a finger. One tooth had been knocked completely out of its socket, the other one broken off into a jagged stump. The numbing pain he'd felt immediately after his collision with the rock was becoming a raw, throbbing ache.

Rose looked at his mouth with the aid of the flashlight and said, "You're fucked up, dude. Damn. With the bald head and bloody mouth you look like an extra from a The Walking Dead. I miss your Bill Hickok look."

Kidd said, "Stop trying to cheer me up," but the way it came out was: "Top twine t' teer me uh."

"Great, a tongue-tied zombie. You need a rag or something to stop the bleeding."

"'Uck it. It-a clot." He removed his torn bomber jacket and pulled his shirt off so Rose could see how badly the troc's talons had mutilated his back.

After a moment she said, "Not too bad. Eight puncture wounds, not much bleeding. Hope those fuckers don't carry killer germs on their claws. We need that first-aid kit."

Feeling suddenly faint, he turned in the driver's bucket seat and eyed the bunk in the trucker's cozy living quarters. "Needa lie 'own 'fore I pass out."

He tried to get up but fell back in the seat. Rose helped him to the bunk, where he collapsed on his back and waited for the world to stop spinning. He shut his eyes.

He was dimly aware of Rose moving around within the truck's cab. After several minutes of flitting about, she said, "Looks like they're gone. Collect yourself, Kidd-O. We have to make a run for it. The clock's ticking and we don't wanna get stuck here until the next full moon."

"Hiding," he said, meaning the trocs. "Waitin' for us. Uh trap."

"Maybe so, but we can't stay here much longer. Get your shit together and let's beat it. Rita can keep 'em off of us. She's already killed a bunch of the fuckers."

He didn't have the energy to argue. His body was betraying him and his mind was muddled. He didn't think he could marshal his waning resolve into action, yet he knew he couldn't let Rose and the others down. "Gimme minute."

Something was happening to him that had little to do with his painful physical injuries. Something he should have foreseen, yes, but what was it? His mind was going mushy. The answer was right in front of him but he couldn't see it because the world was going dark and his thoughts were mired in mental mush.

*   *   *

Several minutes later Rose tried to rouse him. His eyes briefly opened in an ashen face but didn't seem to focus on anything and then they rolled shut. She shook his shoulder. "Wake up, bro," she implored. He didn't.

A shrill whistle drew her attention to the road above. From the driver's-side window she saw Rita with her fingers forked at her lips as she whistled again. Rose rolled the window halfway down and yelled: "What?"

"You have to make a run for it," Rita called. "We'll cover you."

"Kidd's hurt!" Rose shouted. "I can't wake him up!"

Rita and George put their heads together, and a moment later Mallory stepped closer to them, no doubt to put in her two cents' worth of homespun opinion. While they were in roadside conference, Rose went back to Kidd and tried again to wake him. This time his eyes didn't open at all. He was making a gurgling sound that accompanied his stuttering snores, so Rose turned his head to one side so he wouldn't choke on the blood from his split lips and ruined teeth.

She slapped his cheek just hard enough to sting and shouted: "Kidd! William! Wake up, dammit! White Eyes, you sonofabitch! Don't be such a pussy, you hear? WAKE THE FUCK UP!"

No response.

"Come on, dude," she said softly, more to herself than to Kidd, "I don't wanna die in the Big Nowhere. I—"

The jutting rocks interrupted her. The hard ground spoke in a rumbling whisper, and at last she got the message.

She rolled the window wide, stuck her head out and shouted: "We have to get out of here right now!"

Then the earth shuddered and the truck shook and rattled, and Rose knew the ground had spoken the truth. But the truth had come too late.

*   *   *

"No, *I* should go," George said to Rita. "We need you up here with the rifle. I'm not that good a shot."

"You're not in good enough shape to carry him over those damn rocks either," Rita said.

"He's strong as an ox," Mallory said in her portly hubby's defense. "He's not as soft as he looks."

Rita was about to tell them that she could bench-press two hundred pounds—which was a slight exaggeration, since she had maxed out at a hundred and seventy-five—and that she could carry Kidd to safety much faster than George, when Rose shouted that they had to get out of there right now, and then the earth began to tremble beneath their feet.

To Rita, it felt as if giant oceanic waves were rolling under the ground and lifting it up, and she instinctively dropped into a squat, using the rifle's butt to brace herself on the road.

Mallory teetered and fell over backwards. George went down on all fours, a look of panic etched in his cherubic face.

Rita stole a glance at her bike just in time to see it topple over. Then she looked at the Hummer. The wide low-slung vehicle shimmied and bounced on its tires like a toy car.

"Earthquake!" George yelled.

"No shit," Rita said, but her words were lost in deafening thunder as the ground heaved up from below and spilled her headfirst to the edge of the rocky slope.

*   *   *

Facedown on the quaking road, George experienced what he thought must be a religious experience. One moment he felt as insignificant as a flea on the hindquarters of a violently convulsing cur and feared for his pitiful life, but then the next moment came and his fear miraculously left him, and he saw clearly that even if he died here on this unearthly road in an uncharted land that his soul would continue to explore some spiritual geography. He and his team had ridden a mysterious vector into this strange, unstable realm, and whatever might happen next, George knew his spirit would go on—along this road or some other (perhaps ethereal) path—to whatever lay ahead, above, or even behind.

Then the road cracked open with an ear-piercing bang and swallowed him.

*   *   *

Mallory peed in her pants. Whether it was fear that made her lose control of her bladder or the thrashing ground knocking the pee out of her, she neither knew nor cared. Pissy pants were the least of her concern. The only thing that mattered now was living through this bone-rattling disaster and coming out of it more or less in one piece. Flat on her back, the palms of her hands cupped against the gritty road, she sent a jumbled, desperate prayer heavenward—if heaven *was* up there, beyond that fat, too-bright moon which was quickly growing hazy through the quake-spawned dust down here in this hell-on-*un*-earth.

The ground shook coherent thought from her head, and all that was left was the illusion that this place was having its rough way with her, violating her in the worst way, her legs askew and head thrashing, unable to fend off the attack or defend her carnal parts.

She was taking such a savage pounding that she couldn't see George when she tried to turn her head in his direction. The back of her head was getting the worst of it, going rat-a-tat-tat against the road. She did catch a glimpse of that motorcycle woman, though. She was on her hands and knees, riding the edge of the bucking road like some drunk chick trying to ride a giant mechanical bull as she struggled to keep from sliding back down the slope to where the monsters had been and where they might still be lurking.

Mallory wanted to call out to her husband, but her teeth were clenched against the ground's assault and she couldn't make her mouth form a single word.

*   *   *

Until now, Rose had never been in an earthquake. What she knew about quakes had come from textbooks and bloodless lectures. The way this one made the ground roll like waves in the ocean meant they were Rayleigh surface waves, ground roll waves. Powerful ones, guaranteed to do a lot of damage. Their velocity depended on their wavelength. These felt *slow*, which meant they were doing deep damage under the crust, making foundational changes and seriously undermining surface stability.

She lay on top of unconscious Kidd, hugging him to the thin mattress, meaning to keep him safe, to keep him from bounc-ing around like a bare-chested and bloodied baldheaded rag doll. She nuzzled her face into his neck and smelled the copper scent of his spilt blood and the slightly sour musk of his cold sweat. He might've moaned, but the noise of the quake made it impossible to be certain.

"Remember your promise, Brother Owl," she said in the way of a prayer.

CHAPTER NINETEEN

Rita had seen the road break open beneath George Flucker, saw him slide into the jagged fissure's mouth. From where she was hunkered on the road she could still see the top of his head, so she knew he wasn't beyond help, but she couldn't get to him until the ground stopped quaking.

She wished Johnny Headstone were here—still alive and sound of body instead of haunting an empty wheelchair-shrine in a gone-to-shit biker bar—to guide her through this crazy-ass clusterfuck. In lieu of his presence, she imagined the old daredevil was with her in spirit and that was enough to keep her fear in check. *Fear's for pussies*, he whispered in her head. *When the rubber meets the road you got to be ready to explode into right action. No half-ass measures, no hesitation.*

Even when the road is falling apart under you, she added as addendum to Headstone's terse homily.

When Rita was a rookie Rebel Rider under Johnny Headstone's stern auspices, she got into an altercation with a loudmouthed bull dyke in a grungy watering hole on the outskirts of Atlanta's Little Five Points. The mean-drunk dyke was out to prove her ersatz manhood. Rita tried to ignore the dyke's brassy insults. But then: "Hey, biker bitch! I bet you have to tie those long-ass toothpick legs in knots to clear the way to your Glory Hole."

Sitting next to Headstone at the bar, Rita stared at the harsh-faced woman with slicked-back hair, sleeveless T-shirt showing off belligerent tattoos, and scuffed cowboy boots. Rita waited another beat, and then said, "That doesn't *even* make sense. What're you, retarded? Or just stupid drunk?"

The dyke grinned, showing yellow fangs filed to sharp points.

Johnny muttered in Rita's ear, "She's baiting you, Legs. Ignore the ugly cunt."

But then the dyke said, "I'm gonna fuck you up good, bitch. Make you my hog and ride your scrawny ass into the floor."

It was the "scrawny ass" that did it. She turned to Johnny and said, "I don't have a scrawny ass...do I?"

"Hell no," Headstone said, "your ass is *fine*."

Rita slid off the barstool just in time to block a roundhouse right. She threw a counterpunch to the dyke's belly. The bitch doubled over in a perfect setup for a killer uppercut. Rita took her time, lined up the shot, fist to chin, just so, and then she cut loose, putting her weight behind the dynamic lift of the punch and using her strong legs to give the shot devastating power.

It landed squarely on the chin with a hollow pop that sounded like a small-caliber gunshot. The woman's head bobbed while her body tried to decide if it should fall forward or backward, arms hanging apelike and disconnected from the brain. The dyke was lights-out before she crashed forward to the floor.

Rita kissed her throbbing knuckles as the downed dyke's two mannish companions peeled off the bar, cursing and making warlike gestures. One a wiry chick with a blond crewcut and a thin mustache penciled over her lips. The other a stocky brunette, body like a stump, a golden ring through her bovine nose.

"You can take em, Legs," Headstone said with a grin in his tobacco-and-booze-cured voice.

Rita took Crewcut first. She feinted with her fist and then delivered a full-on kick to Crewcut's crotch, the sharp toe of her cowboy boot landing solidly enough to give the bitch fat lips down there. Crewcut yelped, grabbed her crotch and sank to her knees.

Stumpy charged Rita like (what else?) a mad bull and plowed into her midsection, knocking her down and landing on top of her. The woman nuzzled Rita's bosom like a baby rooting for tit. Rita was bra-less under her denim shirt so when Stumpy sank her teeth into breast flesh, just below the nipple, the pain was fierce. Rita sharply slapped her palms against Stumpy's ears. Then she rolled the dazed woman off her, grabbed the ring dangling from her nose and dragged her along the floor until Stumpy was screaming for mercy.

Crewcut was back on her feet, pulling a switchblade. The blade clicked out and she came forward jabbing the air.

Crewcut lunged at Rita's belly, the blade catching nothing but denim. Rita grabbed the neck of an empty bottle from the bar and swung it hard. The bottle struck the dyke's right temple but didn't break. Rita struck again, hammering straight down on Crewcut's forehead. The bottle shattered and the dyke went down, ka-thumping on the floor like a heavy sack of rotting spuds.

To a drunken chorus of catcalls and wolf whistles, Rita unbuttoned her shirt to examine the bite marks on her breast. Then she caught up with the crawling tit-biter and landed three kicks between Stumpy's bovine buttocks. She reached down and ripped the ring from the bitch's nose and flipped it into the air.

The next night, Johnny Headstone took Rita drinking with a good friend of his who was also a very butch dyke. "Just so you know all dykes ain't snappish little shits," he explained.

For a long time after the bar fight, Rita wondered if she would've run from the knife-wielding dyke if Johnny Headstone hadn't been there to see how she handled herself. She finally concluded that she wouldn't have done anything differently in Headstone's absence. Rita Younger was not a cut-and-runner. Her Uncle Renny had once told her that she was distantly related to the infamous Younger brothers who rode with Jesse James. Maybe she was, maybe she wasn't, but when the chips were down, she played her hand as if she was, come holy hell or ass-high water.

Or bone-rattling earthquakes.

The road rolled beneath her and she flattened herself against it with her face resting on crossed forearms. Dust stirred by the quake clogged her nostrils and made her cough. The taste of bitter minerals hung in the back of her throat. She kept her eyes clamped shut to protect them from the harsh particles and earthy effluvium. In the first few seconds of the quake, she'd feared that she was going to die in it, but then she remembered a toothless fortuneteller's prediction that she would not die on any road, and her fear departed, leaving her to ride out the shuddering violence. Sure, it was probably just silly superstition but for now it was enough to hang her hat on.

At last the quaking began to subside, leaving in its wake a few mild tremors that seemed to come along as gratuitous afterthoughts. Rita raised her head and opened her eyes. Moonlit dust hung eerily over the road. The graveyard silence made her shiver.

Then she recalled that George Flucker was caught in a crack in the road and she got quickly to her feet, remembering to pick up the rifle. She went toward the jagged rip running longwise up the middle of the road, but now she didn't see Flucker through the haze of dust.

Mallory was up and talking excitedly, going on about how lucky they'd been to survive, but then she realized George was gone and she commenced to calling upon Jesus and His mother for help. Then she called out to her missing husband.

"He's got his ass in that crack," Rita said, sounding more flippant than she'd intended.

This warranted the full complement of "Jesus, Joseph and Mary" from Mallory.

Down in the rocky Valley of the Baby Beverly dolls, Rose sent up an echoing volley of shouts peppered with profanity.

*   *   *

"Get down here, goddammit, I can't carry this big lug by myself! Hey, hurry up before those fuckers come back!"

The quake was over but Rose was still quaking. Her body tingled, quivering like a newborn calf, but the crucial quaking was occurring much deeper than the under-crust of her skin, along spiritual fault lines. It remained to be seen whether the spirit-quake would leave her soul devastated or set off a transforming upheaval to the good. She figured it could go either way.

In the meantime, she had her hands full with Kidd. He would

not wake up. That was troubling enough, but what really worried her was the spooky look she'd seen in his eyes just before he passed out. It had been in his eyes the first time she ever saw him. A nurse led him by the hand into the group-therapy room and introduced him to the other patients, then she walked him to a chair and sat him down. Rose would've thought he was just another over-medicated, zombified patient but for that look in his eyes—part deer-in-the-headlights wildness, part something else: something wise in the way of mysterious worlds. It was that mystifying thing in his eyes that drew her to him and stimulated some unnamed desire to see what those spooky eyes must've seen. As it turned out, she had met William Kidd as he was beginning to emerge from psychosis mere weeks after his encounter with the uncanny creature that had marked him and inadvertently set him on the road back to relative sanity.

What disturbed Rose now was the idea that Kidd might be going the other way, falling back into his psychosis. Was the stolen road that brought them here also his road back to mind-fucking genetic chaos? Had the troc attack somehow triggered a relapse? Or was it that the cure simply didn't hold in this place? Maybe it was only good so long as Kidd remained back in his home world. Maybe the curative agent the beast had slipped into his system lost its magic here. One more good reason for getting the hell out of here STAT!

She stuck her head out the window again and shouted: "What's the holdup? We need help down here! Hurry the fuck up!"

Looking up at the road, she could see Rita and Mallory but she didn't see George. And Rita and Mallory were ignoring her calls for help.

With a wary glance at the scatter of creepy dolls to make sure they weren't stirring to life, Rose renewed her call for help. Kidd's eyelids fluttered open, then fell shut. He moaned, then was silent.

*   *   *

Rita stood at the edge of the fissure and looked down. There was just enough moonlight for her to see him lying on his back about four feet down at the bottom of the fracture. "George? Stand up and grab hold of the rifle and I'll pull you out," she said.

"Oh God, is he dead?" Mallory moaned.

"Not yet," George grumbled as he got to his feet and reached for the rifle Rita held out for him. "Are you strong enough to pull me up?"

"Yeah, if you use your feet against the side there like you're walking up a wall."

He grabbed hold of the rifle's stock, and Rita planted her feet and leaned backward against his weight. Grunting with effort, he began to walk up the side of the fissure. Mallory held onto Rita's hips to help anchor her, and after a few slips of his feet, George came out of the crack and dropped to his knees on the broken road. Mallory and Rita fell backward on their fannies when he let go of the rifle.

"Thank God," said George, his face a mummer's mask of quake dust. "I thought I was a goner."

Rita jumped up and handed him the rifle. "Cover me," she said. "I'm going to get Kidd."

*   *   *

"Took you long enough," Rose said when Rita reached the truck. She threw open the door and Rita climbed up into the cab.

Rose said, "He's out on his ass and won't wake up."

Rita dragged him off the mattress and to the door. Then she stepped down out of the cab and Rose lowered him into Rita's arms. Rita draped his dead weight over her shoulder and carried him back to the rocky embankment at the foot of the road.

George stood ready with a rope from the Hummer's toolkit. He tossed one end down and Rita tied it around Kidd's chest, under his arms. Rose scampered up the slope to the road and Rita followed. Then the three of them pulled the rope and dragged Kidd up and onto the road.

"How bad is he?" George asked Rose.

She shrugged. "His wounds don't look that bad but something sure knocked him on his ass."

"Let's get him in the Hummer and get the hell out of here," Rita said, glancing at her bike.

"Mallory?" George called. "Where's Mallory?"

"Over there by the Hummer," Rose said with a nod at the vehicle. "What's she doing?"

Mallory stood with her back to them, looking down the road in the direction from which they had come.

"What're you looking at?" Rose asked in a shout.

Mallory slowly turned around. Her round dusted face looked ghostly in the moonlight, but there was no mistaking the mortal terror in her expression. She opened her mouth and tried to speak but no words came out.

"*What?*" George demanded of his wife.

"What's wrong?" asked Rose, growing more anxious by the millisecond.

No longer dumbstruck, Mallory raised her arm, pointed back down the road and said, "We can't go back. The road's split wide open. We… we're stuck here."

CHAPTER TWENTY

"Like hell," Rita said. "We can't be stuck here."

"Look at it!" Mallory pointed again. "Tell me how we can ride across that crack in the damn road. We can't go around it. Not even a Hummer can go over those rocks at such an incline. The road was the only way out of here and now look at it."

Rose stalked off toward the wide rent in the road, stood at its edge and then turned to say: "We'll just have to go on foot around it and then walk our asses out of here."

George said, "I don't think we can. We can't walk sixty miles an hour and I'm pretty sure that's how fast we'd have to go to break out of this place."

"But you don't know that for a fact," Rita said. "And even if it's true, we still have my bike. I can walk it across those rocks and take one of you at a time back to the real world."

"Ferry us across," George mused. "It might work. But we'd better get started right now. The moon is already waning. I think our window of opportunity is about to close. If it hasn't already."

"And that's just a theory too," Rita pointed out. "You don't know for a fact that the moon will close the way home."

"No, but that's how fast we were going to get here in the first place," he said. "And to leave here the first time Mal and I crossed over. Stands to reason…"

"You sure your bike will run?" asked Rose as she glanced at the fallen motorcycle. "The quake could've fucked it up."

Rita walked quickly to her Lowrider and lifted it upright. She climbed into the saddle and tried to crank the engine. It sputtered but the engine didn't start. She tried again. She shut her eyes and willed it to roar to life. It sputtered and nearly caught, but then died. "Come on, dammit, don't fuck with me now. Start!"

It did. She had never felt anything so sweet as the shuddering vibrations she now felt under her rump and between her thighs. "Thank you," she whispered to the Harley as if speaking to a beloved steed.

"Thank you Jesus," said Mallory.

Rita cut off the engine and got off the bike. "All right, who's first?"

Between hacking coughs, George said, "Take Mallory. Please."

Rita nodded. She knew it was the right choice. She saw Mallory as the least resourceful member of the team so it stood to reason she should be the first one out of this damned place. If the monsters attacked again, George and Rose would be better at fighting them off.

Rock dust hung like fog in the acrid air and dimmed the light from the moon, but Rita nevertheless could see the route she should take to get the bike around the long crack in the earth.

"Let's go," she said to Mallory. "I'll need your help getting the bike over those rocks." She pointed to the spot where the drop-off at the edge of the road was shallowest. "That's the way we'll go."

Grim-faced, Mallory nodded. She kissed her husband's lips and then quickly turned away as if to avoid an emotional departure.

"Keep your eyes out for those fucking monsters," Rita said to Rose and George. "They may come back for another go at you."

"Don't worry," George said. "The ground tried to eat me and failed. I'm not about to let those beasties feast on my tender ass."

Holding the reloaded rifle, Rose said, "I'll cover you while you ride out in case they try to stop you."

Rita nodded, thankful that Rose had quickly become a very good shooter. Then she and Mallory started toward the edge of the road, the motorcycle between them.

"You ever been on a motorcycle?" Rita asked Mallory.

"No."

"Nothing to it. You just sit behind me and hold on tight. And pray that we can break out of this goddamn hellhole."

"I already am," Mallory said.

*   *   *

Rose stepped to the edge of the jagged rip in the road and brought the rifle to her shoulder. George was behind her, watching over unconscious Kidd and keeping a lookout for any sign of the trocs' return. Rita and Mallory were on the idling motorcycle on the other side of the second fissure, about fifty yards up the dust-hazed road. Rita raised a fist in the air as if in defiance of hostile gods and then kicked off and gunned the engine. The bike shot forward and Rose said, "Here we go."

"What's that?" George asked.

"Here we go," she repeated, saying it louder this time. "You got my back?"

"Absolutely," he said.

Rose watched Rita and Mallory riding behind the hazy shaft of light from the bike's headlight until they were no longer in sight. She lowered the rifle, a little disappointed that she'd had no opportunity to shoot any interfering trocs. The fuckers must've gone to ground after the quake, she thought.

Then she heard the whispering. Not the rocky earth whispering to her this time. This was something else, the slurping tongue-tied murmuring of a living creature. She leveled the rifle hip-high and looked for the maker of the wet murmurs. Gooseflesh rose on her arms and shoulders. She shuddered inside her coat.

And then she saw the thing raise its head from behind a dark rock. She shouldered her rifle and drew a bead on its white hairless head, centering her aim between two cauliflower-like protuberances she took to be the thing's eyes. The creature kept up its slobbering chatter. Rose didn't know whether to shoot it or ridicule it.

"What *is* that?" George said.

Rose said, "A giant talking maggot?"

*   *   *

"How fast are we going?" Mallory shouted.

"Sixty," Rita shouted back.

The Lowrider was running smoothly and Rita was relieved that it hadn't sustained any quake damage, but the poor visibility worried her. Dust fogged the night air and ate up much of the moonlight and sapped the brightness of the headlight's beam. She couldn't see more than ten yards ahead.

Over the roar of the motor she heard Mallory muttering to herself and realized that she was praying aloud. Couldn't hurt, Rita figured. *If there is a God, we could use a little divine guidance about now. You listening, Big Kahuna? A little help down here?*

The air suddenly changed. Rita was all at once short of breath, as if the atmosphere had grown very thin the way it does at extreme altitudes. Was her cigarette smoking finally catching up with her? No, not likely. It wouldn't come over her this fast. The dust-fog was thinning now, so she didn't think dust was the problem. She could see twenty yards in front of them now, but that was no good if you couldn't catch your breath.

"I can't...breathe," Mallory gasped in Rita's ear.

Rita nodded and cut their speed. Her instinct was that she should turn around and go back the way they'd come, back to where there was enough oxygen to breathe. But that would nix whatever chance they had of getting back to home ground in the familiar world.

The speedometer's needle was falling below forty mph when Rita saw the end of the road.

Not just the end of the road, but the end of this weird world.

She braked and the bike skidded to a stop several feet short of the broken-edged end of the road and the beginning of a great void. It looked as if the land had simply broken off and floated away into starry space. The sensation of being poised at the edge of the planet was dizzying. Though she couldn't breathe, Rita remained there at this impossible precipice, staring into nothingness. Her vision swam with dark shapes and things that weren't quite shapes.

Mallory pinched her. Rita turned the bike around and they rode away fast.

*   *   *

Rose watched in amazement as the maggoty thing crawled out of the crevice and made its way on its belly toward the nearest troc carcass, chattering as it inched its five-foot length along the ground. "That's disgusting," she said. "You smell that thing?"

George Flucker strode to within ten feet of the larval life form, raised his weapon and fired a shot through its head, which exploded, spattering the legs of his pants. An even fouler odor arose from the mushy carnage.

"What the hell'd you do that for?"

"It was disgusting. You said so yourself."

"Yeah but that's no reason to kill it. It wasn't hurting anything."

George shrugged. "We don't know what it would've become. Maggots become flies, but in this place, who knows? You want to tangle with a giant fly? I don't."

Rose saw the sense in what he was saying, but the coldly calculated killing still bothered her. Maybe because the thing had been talking, or at least making noise that sounded like speech. She was wondering what the hell a giant maggot could possibly have to talk about when she heard Rita's motorcycle approaching.

This is it, she thought. *Now we'll know if we're really stuck here.*

But the truth was, she already knew. She was convinced that they would not be leaving this place any time soon. And that there was a good chance they would *never* leave here.

CHAPTER TWENTY-ONE

Mallory wasn't much help with walking the bike back over the rocks, and Rita was exhausted when they rejoined their compatriots. Without a word, Rita sat down on the road, crossed her weary arms on her bent knees and rested her head on her arms. She let Mallory do the talking.

"The road just ends over there," Mallory said with a warbling note of hysteria. "The whole world ends. Just drops off in space. We can't get back."

"Oh shit," said Rose. "I knew it."

"How can that be?" George moved closer to his wife but didn't touch her, almost as if afraid he might become infected with her pessimism. "How can it just end? We were just there an hour ago."

"We're going to die here," Mallory said with a stuttering sob.

Rita raised her head and broke her silence. "With that attitude you probably will. Not me. I've got other plans."

"Plans? What plans?" Rose blurted.

Rita stood up. "Getting out of here alive and back to the real fucking world."

"That's a wish, not a plan," said Mallory.

Rita folded her arms across her chest. "You give up too easy. We'll find a way. Maybe the next full moon the road will come back over there and we can ride out on my bike."

George rubbed his chin and said, "The way this damned road keeps changing, there's no good way to predict what it will do next. Or even where it might take us. Hell, I don't know if it's evolving or devolving."

"Or just fucking with us because it can," Rose interjected.

Then Rita noticed the dead thing in the rocks, just off the road. She pointed a finger and said, "What the hell is that?"

"Fucking giant maggot," Rose answered. "The thing could talk.

But before we could figure out what the hell it was saying, Sir George here killed it, thought it was a white dragon, I guess."

"Not now, Rose," George said. "We've got more important things to deal with."

"Survival," said Rita.

"Yeah," Rose said, "well when our food runs out we might have to eat those big maggots to stay alive. Trocs don't have much meat on 'em. They're all tough hide, stringy muscle and bone, in case you hadn't noticed. These maggot dudes should be tender. Hell, they might not taste too bad roasted over a fire."

'We've got enough food and water to last almost thirty days if we ration it," George said. "Trail Mix and beef jerky, mostly. And dried fruit."

'Yummy," Rose said with a scowl.

"How's Kidd?" Rita asked.

"The same. If he doesn't wake up soon he'll die," said Rose. "Unless you've got IV fluids in that first-aid kit."

"We need to clean his wounds and get proper bandages on him," George said.

"Let's do it," said Rose. "And then get in the Hummer. The longer we stand around here with our asses hanging out, the better the chance the trocs will get us."

Grunting with effort, George carried Kidd over his shoulder and set him down in front of the Hummer so they could dress his wounds by the light of the vehicle's headlights. Rose washed the wounds with peroxide and then applied bandages.

Rita said, "I'm no scientist but I know that you have to go pretty damn high to reach the end of the earth's atmosphere. So how could the atmosphere all of a sudden end there at the end of the road?"

"Gravity holds the atmosphere in place," George said. "I think that's how it works. The higher you go, the weaker gravity gets."

"Well we weren't bouncing around in slow motion," said Rita, "so it wasn't lack of gravity that caused it. So what did? It doesn't make sense."

"Nothing makes sense here," Rose observed. "Not in any way we're used to seeing things. Different laws of science—of physics—apply, otherwise we wouldn't even be here."

Rita chewed her lower lip. Then she said, "I thought I saw something out there where the world stopped. It was there just for a second, then it wasn't. I was so dizzy it might've been a hallucination."

"What did you see?" Rose asked impatiently.

"It looked like a bridge," Rita said. "But it wasn't solid. Like a ghost bridge."

"Ghost bridge," George echoed thoughtfully.

"I didn't see anything," said Mallory.

"Maybe I didn't either," said Rita with a shrug.

"Maybe it was the road back closing down," Rose suggested.

"Well, that's neither here nor there now," said George. "We have to decide what we're going to do. Do we stay here for the next twenty-eight days or do we go exploring down this road?"

"We've been here less than two hours," Rita said, "and we've been through an earthquake and a troc attack. I say we stay on the move and try to be ready for whatever happens next."

"Fine," said George, "but we should wait till sunrise before we go down that road."

"If there *is* a sunrise," Rose said.

*   *   *

Rita sat on the roof of the Hummer and smoked a cigarette. The others were below, trying to catch some sleep in the cramped interior—except for Kidd, who was somewhere beyond sleep. She sent up a silent prayer for him, knowing that she was partially to blame for not keeping the trocs off him. She wondered if prayers could reach God from this fucked up place—assuming God was in his Heaven and all was right with the world. But obviously all was not right with *this* world. *Fuck it*, she decided. *Can't hurt to try.*

The tobacco tasted unusually good. It reminded her of the sweet woodsmoke of a cozy campfire. She inhaled deeply. Blew smoke toward the glaring moon. She smoked the cigarette down to the filter and then flipped the butt to the road. It made sparks when it hit. She counted the smokes remaining in the pack. Thirteen. She would have to make them last as long as she could and then suffer through withdrawal when they were gone.

She glanced down at her bike. She'd parked it beside the Hummer's right front fender so she could keep an eye on it. She didn't know if the trocs were smart enough to try a little creepy-crawly sabotage but she didn't put it past the bastards. If they did, she was ready for them. The rifle had a full load and lay across her lap, ready to rock'n'roll, as Johnny Headstone would've said. The light of that full moon was all she would need to clock any crawlies. But it was getting colder and the winds were picking up. Her jacket wasn't enough to keep her warm out here so she would have to join the others in the vehicle soon. She hated the idea of being packed in like proverbial sardines in that big yellow tin can on wheels but she supposed it would be better than freezing her tits off out in this wind. And in the Hummer she wouldn't have to worry about trocs creeping up and ripping her throat out while she slept.

She huddled deeper in her jacket, determined to remain out here for one more smoke. One more no-worries Slim before the rationing started. She cupped her hands around the Zippo and fired a cigarette.

She stared off down the black road and wondered what lay ahead. Now that the world's end was at their backs.

*   *   *

Sharing a scratchy blanket with Kidd, Rose rested her head on his slack shoulder and wondered where he was, what he was dreaming, and if he would ever come back. And if he did come back, would he come back crazy?

Mallory was already asleep and softly snoring in the front passenger's seat, but George seemed to be having trouble getting comfortable and kept shifting his weight behind the steering wheel, sighing every now and again. Not exactly a picture of conjugal bliss up there in the front seats.

Rose wished Rita would get off the roof and come inside. It wasn't safe out there, not even for a sure-shot badass biker chick. Though Rose didn't think of herself as a lesbian or even bisexual, she did have a crush on Rita, no doubt about it. A chick crush. The woman had some sort of organic magnetism you couldn't resist if you were at least halfway human. Maybe it was an adolescent-like form of hero worship. Whatever it was, Rose felt safe in her company and did not want to lose her.

She listened to Kidd's heartbeat. She wondered if he was dreaming. She put her face inches from his and tried to see if his eyeballs were moving beneath the lids. In the dim light she thought she could see them rolling from side-to-side. So he was dreaming. She knew that guys sometimes got hard-ons when they dreamed so she reached down to Kidd's crotch and felt for an erection. Sure enough, there it was, stiff as a roll of quarters and three times as long. She kneaded it through his jeans, wondering if she might influence his dream. Could she bring him back this way? Grab a guy by the prick, the saying went, and you could lead him anywhere.

She unzipped him and his warm penis fell into her palm.

She put her lips to his ear and whispered: "Dream your way back to me. Rosebud."

*   *   *

Little Billy is nightmaring again. The thing is, the really bad dreams have a way of growing real teeth and claws. The Toad sits behind him, smugly brooding and periodically whip-cracking his tongue to snatch the boy's visions out of the air as fast as they appear. When the Toad speaks it's with a German accent the boy associates with silver screen Nazis fingering flashy cigarette holders. At times like this, Little Billy likes to think of himself as Billy the Kidd because he feels he needs to be tough to survive these brain-to-brain shootouts with the bearded Toad. And because it's better to be a gun-toting outlaw than a nutty fruitcake. The Toad wants to steal Billy's visions and dreams and nail them up on his wall of trophies. The other thing is, the Toad might not be a toad at all—he might be a troll, which would be worse, because trolls eat you alive. Whatever he is, he's off his game today because he is oblivious to what's going on down there under his radar, where the carpet is turning wavy like water and something is breaking the surface and slithering up Billy's leg. He knows it's one of *them*. One of the many monsters that slip into and out of the world through the secret door his mother opened up with her bedtime tales when he was a booger-flicking little kid. The door never closes all the way. It's always ajar. *When is a door not a door? When it's ajar, open to the place where the scariest fairytale fiends live.* He clamps his eyes shut. He doesn't want to see the thing slithering higher up his legs to fondle him and make him hard. He wishes he had the courage to get up and slam that door once and for all and cut himself off from the terrible menagerie of drooling monsters.

"Tell me your dream," the Toad says in his jackboot accent.

What dream?

"The one you are now having."

This is a dream? So I can wake up and this slithery thing won't be fingering my dick?

"Describe it to me."

If this is a dream, then you're not real.

"Oh yes, young man, your dreams are most certainly real. As am I."

You're in my head.

"Yes?"

I can shut you out.

"Perhaps. But I'm not your problem, am I?"

He breaks off the dialogue. He knows his problem is the creature coiled around his penis, working it with rough strokes. He knows he has to find a way out of this dream but he doesn't want that stroking to stop. The only thing to do is give in to it. After that, who knows? He might wake up or he might sink deeper into this illicit delirium. It's out of his hands.

*   *   *

His penis was weeping in her hand and Rose knew he was getting ready to blow. What if, she wondered, it shoots up and smacks George in the back of the head or spatters up there on the windshield. *Can't have that. This is our moment. Mine and Kidd's and no one else's.* She bent down and took him in her mouth. Several beats later he flooded her mouth as she moved her lips up and down his shaft.

Then he screamed.

*   *   *

When she heard the scream Rita threw down her half-smoked cigarette, slid off the Hummer's roof and landed nimbly on her feet. She brought the rifle to her shoulder as she spun around to look for a target—a troc that had somehow gotten at somebody inside. The dome light came on and she saw Kidd sitting upright in the backseat with his eyes wide and a look of terror on his face. No troc. George and Mallory had turned in their seats and were staring with surprised expressions at Kidd's crotch. Then Rita saw Kidd's glistening erection and said, "Jesus!"

Wiping her lips, Rose was trying to calm him, saying, "It's all right, it's all right. You're cool. Easy bro. It was just a bad dream. A wet one."

Rita retrieved her cigarette from the road and took a deep draw. She tapped the rifle's barrel on the window glass and said, "You're lucky I didn't blow that thing away, Kidd. Put it back in your pants."

Kidd flung his door open and jumped out of the vehicle. He teetered as if the earth were still quaking, then he fell against the Hummer and sank to the hard ground. Rose jumped out behind him and bent to try to pick him up.

"Well it worked, didn't it?" Rose said. "I snapped him out of it."

"You mean you snapped *it* out of *him*?" Rita waved her weapon at Kidd's flagging erection.

His eyes were still wide-whites but Rita wasn't sure he was back with them. "Kidd? You here? Say something."

"Dark…" he said, then mumbled something about her motorcycle.

"He's not really with us," Rita said. Then she reached down and pulled him to his feet. With a businesslike manner, she stuffed his penis back in his pants and zipped him up. Then she looked at Rose and said, "What were you thinking?"

Rose worked her mouth but couldn't seem to find the words.

Rita said, "Never mind, I don't want to know. Help me get him back in the vehicle."

CHAPTER TWENTY-TWO

Kidd dreamed he was waking. Awaking from a dream he didn't want to have because it was too strange, too dark, too thundery with motorcycles and monsters. He was with friends, faces familiar and some less so, though certainly not unfriendly. But the faces kept fading into darkness, and the ozone stink of this dangerous dreamland jumbled his mind and made him too clumsy for the mental acrobatics he was used to, or *used* to be used to. And the voices. Murmuring magpies with human heads and sinister feathers fanned in front of their faces as if hiding true identities. Feather dancers. He wished they would all just fly away and leave him alone. He had something to do. Something important but there were too many distractions and he couldn't think what it was he should be doing. But if he didn't pull it off, bad things would happen. People would die. He would die. Was that right? Yes, it had to be. It was up to him to set things right, to save lives, to keep the encroaching darkness at bay, at least long enough to set up proper defenses against the invaders and interlopers and intransigent evildoers. Because…

"Kidd! Open your eyes, goddammit! Stay with us!"

"Wha—" he said, but his voice had a kind of echo now, chasing itself around and around inside a deep chasm. But there was another sound too. That deep hum coming from nowhere and everywhere, felt more than heard, changing pitch at regular intervals, mathematical rhythms reaching deep into his belly.

WOOOO-AHH WOOOO-AHH WOOOO-AHH

He realized he'd been hearing this mysterious hum for as long as he could remember. But it had remained mostly sub-audible, below his conscious notice. The image of the earth as a giant humming machine came into his thoughts. Electromagnetic music. Music of the spheres?

Sound and quiet fury. Signifying…what? Listen long enough and you aren't sure it isn't coming from you—your own body's electromagnetic music, biologically disharmonic and offbeat.

He gave himself to the duotone hum and sank deep into the dream, deeper into himself, closer to a dark door marked DREAMING. A freestanding iron door hanging on nothing but mist. The lettering began to glow in the iron as the door swung open.

Kidd glided inside.

*   *   *

Rose didn't try to defend her actions. She did what she did for Kidd, not for them. He was her blood brother and that was all that mattered. She owed them no explanation. Too bad it hadn't worked better. Kidd shot his wad and came out of his trance only briefly, then went back under, back below the surface of whatever dream pool he was stuck in.

The Fluckers were already settling down for sleep in the front of the Hummer, George beginning to snore. Rita was still outside, smoking the last bit of her retrieved butt.

Rose wished she could sleep but she was too hyped now. Too antsy-dancy. She needed something to read to make her sleepy. Then she remembered the spiral notebook in Kidd's hip pocket. He had flipped through the pages when he first found it and said it looked like the trucker had used it as a journal documenting his *lost road* experience here in the Big Nowhere. Was it still there?

It was. She took her penlight from her shoulder bag, flicked it on and opened the notebook. It was printed neatly in a very precise hand and easy to read.

Rose read.

Day 1

A nightmare. Don't know what happened or how. Thank God Angel is ok. Just scared. Me too. Those damn things out there want to get at us. So far we're safe. If they don't break the windows and drag us out of the truck. What the hell are they? Like no animal I've ever seen. At least a dozen of them.

Showed up right after the crash.

Crash—still don't know how it happened. SUV passed me and for no reason was suddenly all over the road and I braked hard to avoid hitting it when it jammed on its brakes. Then I was off the road and there was a god-awful roar like a tornado and then I was out, knocked cold but just for a minute or two, Angel says. And we ended up here in this rocky place but nowhere near where I ran off the road. Cell phone useless—no signal. CB radio nothing but static. Can't raise anybody. And these freaky creatures won't give up and go away. Got my Glock 19 with a full clip and a box of Blazer Brass ammo so I can shoot these critters if I have to but how many more might be out there in those weird red rocks?

We ate snacks and Angel napped but I stayed awake watching those monsters watching us.

Day 2

We have bottled water, a sixpack of Coke, candy and crackers but not enough to last more than a couple more days. Hoping somebody will see us down here but don't even know where here is. Nothing familiar here. Like a UFO snatched us off the road and dropped us on some other planet. Unbelievable but here we are. Angel's getting antsy. Poor kid freaked out by these alien looking creatures. We use empty water bottles to pee in. Being a girl, Angel has a hard time hitting the target. So far we're too scared to poop. Might be funny some day but this ain't that day. Scared shitless for real.

Getting worried now. We can't stay here much longer. Don't know what's out there or how far we can get. Guess that's why I'm writing this. If we don't make it maybe somebody will find this notebook. I took photos of the Slinkers (as Angel calls em) with my phone but I'm taking it with us when we go. It has to work somewhere—if we're not on some other damn planet.

Day 3

Angel woke me up screaming. Bad dream. I got her quiet but we're still stuck in this bad dream. She pooped herself. Poor kid. Rolled window down just a crack to toss her panties out. One of the Slinkers grabbed it and licked the shit, didn't like it and threw it down.

Bad news. One of them picked up a rock and came at us like he wanted to break the window. I opened it just enough to shoot at him. Scared him off. But they're not just dumb animals. They can use rocks as tools, a sure sign of higher intelligence.

Angel wants me to sound the horn to scare them off. Not a bad idea but will wait on that. Save it for the right time. Probably only work the first time. After that they won't be scared. Just pissed off.

There seems to be more of them at night so daytime will be best for making a run for it. I'll shoot as many as I can then we will go. First I have to get Angel psyched for it. I told her the plan and she panicked, freaked out bad and I don't think I can get us out of here safe if I have to drag her kicking and screaming.

3 of the monsters started playing a game with one of the dolls from my spilled cargo, kicking it and throwing it. Reminds me of Internet vid of jihadists playing soccer with severed heads. I don't like it. These things are smarter than their lizard looks would make you think.

Day 4

This is it. We go today. Snacks are all gone and most of the water. Angel is as ready as she's going to be. It's morning and I count 8 of them scattered around in loose formation, waiting. Can't see how many behind the truck.

Here's the plan. I open the driver-side door's window and shoot any on that side so I can open the door and shoot the ones in front or behind. Angel will be watching and if they start coming at me to attack she will start blasting the horn to startle them. I'll shoot until I have to reload, then duck back inside, reload and repeat until they're all dead or fled. Then we will get the hell out of this damned gorge and hike back to the world.

God be with us.

I shot one! It came at the windshield with a rock, jumped up on the hood. I threw the door open leaned out and shot it in the chest. Then slammed the door just before another one could get at me. The one I hit fell on the ground writhing and then went still. Then the others grouped around the dying one like a weird ceremony for last rites. If they're scared of my gun they don't show it. Angel freaked again. Started crying when I shot the thing but I talked her down and her crying turned to laughing. Not sure how she'll be when it's time to run for it. But we can't wait. We go now.

She's gone. My little girl. Something big came out of the sky and took her up. I have to find her. Took her west.

God help me. And my Angel.

Rose sat straight up, pounded a fist on the ceiling of the Hummer and shouted: "Rita! Get your ass in here now! They come out of the sky!"

"You scared the shit out of me," the Flucker woman said in a sleepy voice. "Stop yelling."

Rita was at the back window, saying "What the hell are you talking about?"

Undismayed, Rose said, "It's right here in the trucker's diary. Something came down and snatched his kid and flew off with her."

"Oh my God," George said.

"I bet it's those giant talking maggots," Rose said, "what they turn into, like big-ass fly beasties."

"She's right," George said to Rita. "You'd better get in here now."

Rita said, "Just when you think things can't get any worse. Wish I'd brought my shotgun."

*   *   *

Kidd fell through the fog. And kept falling. Finding no ground. And then he was flying. Actually flying through the air. Climbing, soaring, gliding on thin currents. Amazingly liberating. *Flying.*

The hum was beneath him now, down there somewhere on the ground. A faint *wooo-ahhh wooo-ahh*. Down there with his worldly cares—or otherworldly cares, in this case, in this place—down there with Rose and Rita and the Fluckers. The valley of the dolls and carnage, the quaking rocks and vicious trocs.

Above all that.

Flying.

But he was not alone up here. As he broke through blinding clouds, the sky filled with flying monsters. And he was all at once falling, hurtling toward the ground with monsters chasing him down to his certain death.

*   *   *

Rita crowded into the vehicle and sandwiched herself between Rose and Kidd. "This is a big fucking can and we're the fucking sardines," she said.

"Yeah but those flying fuckers out there like to eat sardines," Rose opined. "So relax and enjoy our big fucking can."

Rita gave her a hard look, then closed her eyes for some hoped-for sleep in this cursed place.

Kidd moaned and whimpered in his sleep, and then his body twitched as if something had suddenly grabbed him.

CHAPTER TWENTY-THREE

Kidd woke to a startling commotion. He opened his eyes. The padded cage he was in was rocking, gently bouncing. The things packed in beside him looked like familiar people but he knew he couldn't trust appearances now. These "people" could be monsters wearing human skin. Rip off the human layer and you would see the pebbled hide of a troc—or worse. He had to get out of this upholstered cage.

"Kidd, you with us?" the female on his left said.

"Welcome back, asshole," said the other familiar female. "How're you feeling?"

The back of the monster's head in front of him rose up from a slouched position and the head spoke in a sleepy voice: "What's going on?"

The second monster up front in the cowboy hat and the woman's body said, "Is it morning yet? I'm hungry."

"Kidd, what're you doing?" the closest female asked him.

"Gotta get out," he mumbled as he reached for the door handle.

"Dude, out where? It's not safe out there."

The words were out of his mouth before he could stop them: "Not safe in here."

He popped the door open to climb out, then fell to one knee on the ground. The sky was brightening, going from goose gray to deep plum purple (but rather more like the color of a deep bruise). There was an ozone scent in the chill air. The atmosphere seemed charged with pre-storm energy, as if tornadic spirits were spinning up deadly mischief nearby.

Kidd shivered. He stood. He hugged himself against the chill.

The tall female jumped out of the boxy vehicle. He was supposed to know her name but it escaped his dizzy memory for the moment.

"Kidd," she said, "are you all right? Everybody's worried about you since that thing tore into you. You've been pretty much out of it. What's going on?"

"Got to get out of this place."

"No shit. If you've got any bright ideas about how to do that in that mega-smart brain of yours, let's hear it."

He looked into her eyes, which reflected the purple sky, now glowing scarlet around the edges of the horizon. "I know you," he said.

"Well duh. Of course you know me. What do you…? Kidd, what's my name?"

He stared silently into her eyes, watching them turn red.

"Say my name." She touched his arm.

Then it came back to him and it tripped from his tongue: "Rita."

"Bingo. Give the man a cigar and a blowjob." She gave him a wary crooked half-smile, the way you might look at a dog you suspected of being mad.

His face scrunched itself up in confusion. "A blowjob?"

"Jeez, Kidd, you used to have a sense of humor. What the hell happened?"

He shrugged. He wanted to trust this woman, wanted to believe there was not something hideously dangerous hiding beneath her skin.

"I don't know what's real," he said. "I see things I can't trust to be true. I don't see things that…might be hiding from truth. I want to trust you. But I can't be sure."

"How long have you known me?"

"I don't know. How long is long?"

"I don't know, Kidd. How high is high? How fucked is fucked? *We* are. Fucked. We need that brain of yours on-track to help us figure out how to get out this fucked up place. Okay?"

"I think I'm supposed to be here."

"I don't think anybody's supposed to be here," she said. "It's some kind of accident of nature."

"Or super nature."

"That or some big fucking cosmic accident of the universe. Whatever it is, it's fucked and we need to get unfucked and get the fuck out of here. So shape up, will you? Your friends need you in fighting trim."

He gave her a noncommittal shrug, then looked off into the sky where dawn should be breaking soon. He shivered.

"You've known me long enough to know you can trust me," she said. "You still can. Trust me. Are we good?"

"Good," he echoed.

"Good." She looked off down the dark road ahead of them. "Now how the hell can we get out of here with our asses intact?"

"Not sure we're supposed to."

"Don't say that shit. That's fatalistic as fuck."

"Maybe not you. But *I'm* supposed to be here. I have the mark. They own me." He touched the scar under his eye.

"Bullshit, Kidd. A minute ago you said we shouldn't be here. You're confused. Snap out of it!"

A metallic click and thud echoed off the surrounding rocks and here came another female falling out of the big boxy cage on wheels. The one called Rose. Or Rocky. His *blood sister*. Unless it was a monster wearing Rose's skin. "Had to get outta there," she said. "Those two arguing over crazy shit. Cowgirl's all like, I wish we could go find a fast food McBreakfast and he tells her eat the trail mix, she could stand to lose a few pounds. Then she tells him to eat shit."

"Ain't marriage grand," Rita said with a scowl.

"And here comes Cowgirl," Rose said. "It's like a big yellow clown car and the clowns just keep piling out.

With her straw cowboy hat scrunched low and angrily over her eyes, the Flucker woman said, "That man makes me so mad I could spit."

"Hell, that ain't what I call very mad," Rose said.

"Spit in his eye, then. Is that better?" The woman cut her eyes at Rose. "Does that make you happy?"

"Hey, I don't care what you do to him. He ain't exactly proved himself all that useful here in the Big Nowhere. Not that it's his fault for getting his ass in a crack when the ground tried to swallow him."

Kidd tuned the chattering females out. He stared into the lightening sky where he saw something moving. A lot of somethings. He raised his arm and pointed his finger like a pistol. "Look there."

"Huh?" Cowgirl looked at Kidd.

"What is that?" Rose looked at the sky. "That's—holy shit!"

"A giant flock of birds. Or a flock of giant birds," Rita observed.

"You sure it's birds and not those troc things with wings?" Cowgirl asked, her voice shaky with something more than anger now.

The back of Kidd's neck bristled and he touched the scar under his eye. It was itching but no longer twitching. "Crows," he said. "Big ones."

"Holy shit," Rose said. "Hundreds of those fuckers. And they're coming this way."

"Back in the car!" Rita shouted. "Quick!"

"They won't hurt us," Kidd said. "They're going after *them*." He pointed to a different part of the sky.

"Whoa, dude! What the fuck!" Rose said when she saw *them*. "I *knew* it. What those giant maggots turn into. Flying fucking trocs! But that's a mega murder of crows! How do you know it's not us they want to murder?"

"I just know," he said. "Like they're under my skin, the crows."

Rita said, "Never mind the crows, what about those flying trocs?"

"I only see three," Kidd said. "Crows will either kill them or scare them off."

"How do you know that?" Rita asked.

With a shrug he said, "I just do."

"Holy guacamole," the priestly Flucker said when he got out of the vehicle and saw the sky full of flying creatures.

A handgun appeared in Rita's hand, her eyes locked on the sky. Kidd knew then that this was the real Rita, not a monster-in-hiding imposter. This was the former biker chick that rode a vintage Harley and kicked ass like a man. And it was probably not a good idea to call her *chick* to her face. Kidd chilled out a little as his paranoia backed off enough so that he could breathe easier. He could feel the jumbled pieces of his psyche settling back into place. Or trying to.

The trio of winged trocs split up, each going its separate way to divide the pursuing flock of crows. Pretty smart, Kidd thought. But not likely to save the trocs from what was winging after them like a black-feathered tornado. The massive tornado of crows divided into three smaller twisters, each one chasing a different troc. Against the slowly reddening sky, the aerial display was ominously apocalyptic.

Kidd and the others watched in silence as one by one the trocs were overtaken and brought down by perfectly choreographed attack formations.

When all three trocs were on the ground, scrums of enormous crows ripped and shredded their reptilian skin, tearing the trocs apart, some of the birds taking back to the sky with a pieces of troc in their beaks.

Rose said, "Crows back in the real world are nothing like these big fuckers."

Kidd nodded. "And their midair mobbing is not as coordinated as these here."

"He's back," Rose said. "The know-it-all Kidd knows his crows. Welcome back, dude."

The crow detachments on the ground took to the air with military precision now that the trocs had been decimated. Then the black thunderhead of crows flew off into the glowing sky.

"That was amazing," George Flucker said. "but let's not hang around here for whatever this place throws at us next. Let's get down that road to see where it goes. No future here, and there could be another quake any time."

His wife said, "I don't think we should get too far from where we came into this world. We may never get back home."

"That way's already closed behind us," Rita said. "You saw it yourself."

"She's right," George said. "There is only one way to go. The ground is too rough and rocky to go off-road here. The road ahead."

Rose asked the question for which no one had an answer: "And if we run out of road?"

CHAPTER TWENTY-FOUR

"So those lizard-like creatures have wings and can fly here," George Flucker said, "but you've never seen the flying kind back in our world?"

Kidd shook his head, his eyes still on the sky.

Flucker's wife said, "Like flying monkeys in Oz."

"But shit scarier," Rose said.

Rita said, "Those three dead ones don't look so scary now. They look like roadkill on the devil's road to hell."

Rose touched Kidd's arm. "You see something up there? Why're you staring at the sky?"

"Stars. Planets. They're fading now because dawn is coming but you can still make out a few constellations."

"Yeah, so?"

"So it's backwards. It's pointing the wrong way. Like a mirror image of the sky we know. You can find the North Star using the Dipper as a pointer but here Polaris seems to be missing altogether."

"So the sun's going to rise in the west and set in the east?" Rose scrunched up her face.

Kidd shrugged. "Something like that, I guess. I can't quite figure it out. It almost makes sense but not really. Like different laws of science are at work in this place."

"Yeah, that's pretty fucking obvious." Rose said.

"Time to go, folks," George said. "We can eat on the way."

"Yeah, but on the way where?" Rose said.

"All roads lead to one place," Kidd said, his eyes finally drifting away from the fading stars.

"Yeah, and where might that be, bright boy?" Rita asked, her face serious. Was she blaming him for getting her into this one-way trip deep into desolation?

"The end," Kidd said.

"Well aren't you a bundle of optimism," Cowgirl Flucker said, pushing her hat higher on her head and pulling a long face.

"He's more fun when he's batshit crazy," Rose said, "but he's usually right about how shit works. Or works out. Or doesn't."

Kidd ran a hand over his shaved head, making sure it was still there, still reduced to bristles. He couldn't shake the feeling that he was changing from the inside out in some occult metamorphosis.

"Let's go if we're going," Rita said. "Jacking our jaws ain't getting it done."

"Maybe you shouldn't ride your bike, what with those flying troc things," George suggested. "One could come along and snatch you off."

"I'll take my chances mounted up," she said, patting her holstered pistol, "and staying vertical."

"Rock on!" Rose raised a hand with fingers making heavy-metal horns. Unless it was a salute to Satan.

*   *   *

The sky went from purple to pink and finally to a dingy blue-gray. There was no sun in sight, though the sky didn't appear to hold any clouds. The Fluckers were sitting in the Hummer, talking or arguing. Rita was fiddling with her Harley. Rose noticed that Kidd kept glancing nervously up at the sky. She was still worried about his mental state and didn't believe he had fully returned to his normal frame of mind, though she was pretty sure he was no longer out there dangling at the end of his psyche's tether. He was rebounding but he wasn't all the way back just yet. But would his rebound overshoot his default setting and take him into some other extreme?

"See something, bro?" she asked with a gentle touch on his arm.

"Don't see," he said. "The sun. Night gave way to day but where's the light coming from? Shouldn't the sun be up there by now?"

Rose shrugged. "This is one strange place, dude. Don't waste your time trying to make sense of it. Shit here ain't like shit back home. Concentrate that laser of a brain on how we can get the fuck out of this place. When we get back to the world, then you can wrack your brain and figure it all out."

He said nothing back. Just kept close watch on the drab and dreary sky and its vaulting emptiness.

Rose thought she should try to keep him anchored on the ground so she attempted to engage his attention. "What happened back there in the backseat—I didn't mean to freak you out. I thought I could snap you out of your Crazy Train ride by pulling your pud. I'm not a sexual predator, you know that. Right?"

He looked at her with big eyes as they stood in the middle of the primitive road. "That was you?"

"Well, yeah. Who'd you think?"

"I thought it was a monster. I was dreaming or hallucinating. Or both."

"Sorry, Kidd. I was just trying to help. Not saying I didn't enjoy it though. Until you screamed."

"I screamed?"

"Oh yeah. You creamed and screamed, my brother. Hot, thick and loud. You're welcome."

"Sorry," he muttered.

"Hey, no sweat. It worked, didn't it? I brought you back. Mostly back. You are back, right?"

"In my right mind?" Now he shrugged. "Nothing feels right in this place."

Rose gave him a lopsided grin. "But you know what? I'm almost beginning to like it here. In a crazy-ass kind of way. I mean, look at these rocks! This landscape. Never seen anything like it. I want to get the hell out of here but I'm not sorry we came. I'll be sort of sorry to leave. But we'll never get out of here if you light out for La-La Land again."

"Uh-oh," one of the Fluckers said. They were out of the vehicle and were standing several paces behind Rose and Kidd, who both turned to see what the *uh-oh* was about.

"They're back," George said, pointing at the sky behind them.

"Those crows."

Kidd clawed at his troc mark to scratch its sudden intense itching but it didn't do much to ease the itch.

Rita straddled the Harley and said, "Time to go if we're going, kids. Keep moving. Don't give the enemy a stationary target."

"Right," Rose said. "Sitting ducks get plucked."

Then she looked at Cowgirl and said, "You *don't* wanna be a plucked Flucker."

Cowgirl screwed up her face into an expression of sour sarcasm. "Do you have to always be running your smart mouth?"

Rose opened her mouth but nothing came out, as if suddenly dumbstruck.

"Mount up and move out," Rita said in ironic imitation of a battle-field commander. The Rebel Rider was eager to spur her steel horse.

Everyone but Kidd was eager to follow her barked order. He stood statue-still.

Rita's Harley rumbled and roared and seemed as eager as she was to ride out. "Kidd! Let's go!" she shouted above the bike's raucous grumble.

He made to follow the others into the Hummer, saying as he moved: "The crows are using us as bait. I think they're providing us escort."

"Hoping we'll draw more monsters as we go. Yes, that does make sense," George said as he sank into the driver's seat.

"That's fucking great," Rose said. "We're the bait and this road is the hook."

"Maybe the crows will scare any trocs away?" Cowgirl said, her inflection rising at the end to make her statement an interrogative.

"Unless there are too many trocs," Rose said, refusing to be un-duly optimistic. "Then there's a big-ass battle and we're the fucking battleground when the attack comes."

CHAPTER TWENTY-FIVE

Rita rode ten yards or so ahead of the Hummer, whose speed George kept under 20 mph, despite Rita's frustrated exhortations to move at a faster clip. Kidd sat in the back with Rose on his right. He did his best to keep his weight off the wounds he'd received in what they all by general agreement already referred to as the Battle of the Valley of the Dolls, but his wounds nevertheless kept up a constant dull ache that seemed to go deep into his bones. Overnight Mallory Flucker had become Cowgirl, a moniker she didn't seem to much mind, or if she did, she kept further protestations to herself. Like a little sister playing big sister, Rose kept a close eye on Kidd, wary of whatever was going on inside him. She made it clear that she felt responsible for his wellbeing. As for her own state of mental health, she seemed genuinely unconcerned, as though she had already conquered her demons, imaginary and otherwise, nor did she expect to have to reengage any such bugaboos except "those ugly fucking troc motherfuckers"—which were anything but imaginary.

"Why are you watching me like a hungry hawk?" Kidd asked when Rose eyeballed him once too often.

"I'm your *blood sister*. It's my job."

"Well cut it out or you'll be out of a job. You're making me paranoid. Like something's wrong with me."

"Face it, bro, since we've been here you've lost your luster as poster boy for reconstructed psychos. No offense. Your mind has lost some of its bright healthy shine and now there's a dull coat of crazy."

"How about you? Does being here somehow boost your vocabulary? You're using words and phrases outside your bailiwick and out of character for the young rebel rock-hound bohemian we all know and love. *Lost your luster*? You don't talk like that."

She shrugged and rolled her eyes. "I got your bailiwick right here," she said, grabbing at her crotch. "I picked up a lot of boring hifalutin shit from shrinks and such. And I did do some college, remember. Sometimes shit like that just pops out before my mouth knows what it's saying. And hanging out with your brainy ass exposes me to those rich nuggets that spew from your mouth."

"Well just stop worrying about me. I'm okay. I—"

Something in the atmosphere changed; the light beneath the sunless sky wavered as if someone were playing with a dimmer switch, the earthy scent of the air suddenly turned metallic, and that ever-present sub-audible hum deepened, then grew steadily in volume, rising in pitch until it was virtually shrieking.

"Earthquake!" George shouted, his voice cracking like a teenager's.

"No," Rose said. "That's something else!"

"Then what—" Cowgirl began, her voice edged with hysteria.

As if in answer to her unfinished question, the short stretch of road between the Hummer and Rita's bike blurred, falling out of focus as if it were no more than a mere projection. Rita all but disappeared, eclipsed by whatever was materializing directly in front of the Hummer.

"—is that?"

"Holy fuck," Rose said, gawking at the thing taking shape before them.

George jammed his foot on the brake pedal and the Hummer lurched to a halt.

A black van swerved left then right as it took the road in front of them. Its windows were tinted, its occupants invisible. The van righted itself and rolled to a stop fifteen or twenty yards ahead.

"I can't see Rita," Rose said. "What the fuck!"

"This could be a good thing," George offered. "If this van just came from back in the world, then maybe this is our way out. This stretch of road."

"There." Kidd pointed ahead. "There she is."

Rita had turned around and was riding back this way, apparently having heard and seen the van appear on this unearthly road. She rode quickly past the black van and didn't slow down until she was well behind it. Then she rolled to a stop, got off the bike with her pistol in her hand.

"Smart," Kidd said. "Since we have no idea who's inside that van, she flanks it so she doesn't make herself a potential target."

"Target? Why would she be a target?" Cowgirl asked.

"Anything's possible," Kidd said. "Caution is key."

"We can't let Rita take 'em on by herself," Rose said. "Everybody out. Let's go."

Rita rapped on the back of the black van and held her gun high, pointing at the empty sky. "Come on out!" she shouted.

Nobody came out. Rose, Kidd, George and Cowgirl piled out of the Hummer. Rita hit the van again, this time with the barrel of her pistol. "Come on out, we need your help."

The side door of the van slid open and a tall man in a hooded indigo robe stepped down onto the road. Right behind him, a second robed figure hopped out, this one a thin girl whose blonde hair was just visible inside her own indigo hood, quickly followed by a third smaller person robed in the same deep blue-purple radiance.

Rita holstered her pistol and gave the robed trio her tough biker bitch stare.

"What the fuck?" Rose said.

"Where are we?" the small one asked in a high-pitched cartoon-ish voice.

The tall indigo-robed guy's voice was deep and mellow when he said, "Who are you people." The way he said it, it sounded more like a command than a question.

"Holy crow shit!" Rose said, raising a finger to point at the colorful artwork painted on the side of the van in bold realistic detail. "You guys seeing this shit?"

Kidd addressed the tall man, keeping his voice soft and nonthreatening: "Would you mind closing the van's door so we can see the rest of what's painted there?"

The man didn't answer but continued to stare into Kidd's face, studying him closely, as if he recognized him but wasn't sure from whence he had come.

"Please," Kidd said, insistence lending his voice firmness.

The tall man turned, seized the door handle and slammed the van's door shut with a hollow click that echoed oddly off the rocky terrain.

"You've been here before?" George asked the newcomers.

"Only in dreams," the tall one answered, pushing back his hood to reveal a polished skull completely bereft of hair.

The painting covering the side of the van was a panoramic view of the otherworldly place in which they all now found themselves. Beneath the image in bold lettering the same indigo as the van voyagers' robes were these word: THE END OF THE ROAD.

"That's the Big Nowhere," Rose said. "That's this place right where we're standing. No shit, it is."

The tall man said, "No shit, indeed."

CHAPTER TWENTY-SIX

"I'm Brock," the tall bald man said as he turned back to Kidd. His eyes were a blue not quite as intense as their indigo robes but didn't miss by much. His strong jawline sported flaxen stubble that gave him the appearance of a pretty-boy fashion model who had skipped shaving for a couple of days, going for the ruggedly handsome look.

Kidd didn't like the way the guy was staring at his face. Rose noticed it too, touched Kidd's arm and said, "What is this, a skinhead reunion?" Then she playfully Buddha-rubbed Kidd's shaved head. "Long lost brothers?"

"You have the totem mark," Brock said to Kidd. "The scar under your eye."

"What do you know about it?" he asked.

"I've seen it in a dream. But I didn't see the animal that gave it to you. Just its claws."

"It was a vision," the blonde in the robe said. "Brock is like our shaman? Sometimes visions come to him in dreams. I'm Miranda."

Rose said, "I'm Rose but you can call me Rocky. Totem boy here is Kidd with two d's. This here's Rita our badass biker babe, and that's Cowgirl there and her husband Father George, our fallen priest."

Cowgirl tipped her hat and said, "My name's Mallory, not Cowgirl."

George said. "And I was never a priest."

"You might've been if you hadn't fallen in with Cowgirl." Rose winked, then she pointed at the short, robed figure and said, "That your kid?"

The small person pushed back the hood, which had almost completely hidden his face and said, "I'm not a kid. I am as you see."

"Oh, you're a midget," Rose said with an ah-ha nod as she took in his worry-lined forehead and scarred jaw.

The little man scowled and said, "I believe the word you're looking for is *dwarf*."

The dwarf had a scrubby moustache over a tight mouth and dark eyes that looked too big for his face. The moustache was reddish, his skin alabaster.

Rose made a noise like a game-show buzzer: "The word I'm looking for is Munchkin."

The dwarf scowled. The lines on his high forehead deepened in shadow. His eyes widened as if to take in the entirety of Rose's personhood. "You're an abrasive bitch, aren't you."

Her face flushed with scarlet heat. "Watch your mouth or I'll go full-on abrasive upside your head with this rock hammer."

"Enough," said Brock the alleged shaman. "We are all here in this sacred place by design, not accident. There is no need to fight it. We have come here to accept our fate."

Kidd nodded at the words on the side of the van and said, "'The end of the road'—that's your version of *the end is near,* right?"

"Something like that, though ours is much more apropos, as you can see by looking around you."

George said, "You're a doomsday cult."

"Like that Heaven's Gate bunch?" Cowgirl said. "That killed themselves so that comet would carry their souls to heaven or some such nonsense? Good Lord!"

Brock's eyes danced in their sockets and reflected the eerie glow of the rocky surroundings. He said, "Neither good nor bad is the so-called Lord."

Clearly growing impatient with the bullshit banter, Rita said, "If it's the end of the road you're here for, follow this road right behind us and you'll see the real thing. You can drive right off into end of the fucking world. But unless you guys know how to get back to where you just came from, you're in our way and wasting our time with your blue robes and bullshit."

George said, "You're missing the point. Don't you see? If these guys entered this place here then maybe we can get out of here the same way they came in. We can back up far enough to get up to sixty miles an hour and make our exit. We have to try. Right now. Let's go. Before it closes."

Rita shrugged. "What do you think, Kidd?"

"It might work," Kidd said. "But I'm not sure we're supposed to leave yet. We must be here for a reason."

"What reason?" George pressed him. "Our mission now is finding a way back home. I for one don't want to die in this place. The longer we stay here, the less our chances of surviving."

"Sounds right to me," Rita said with a nod to George. "Let's do it."

"Hell yeah," Cowgirl agreed, already walking toward the Hummer.

"Hold on," Kidd said. Then he addressed Brock, the apparent leader of the van people: "Why *did* you come here? What exactly do you intend to do now that you're here?"

"Who cares?" Rose threw up her hands. "If they wanna end up as human communion wafers for the trocs, that's no skin off my ass. Let's just get the hell outta here."

"Trox?" Brock echoed.

"That's what we call the beasts that have the run of this place," Kidd said. "I guess you didn't see them in your, uh, visions."

Brock nodded. "Like the one that marked you."

"For Christ's sake, people, let's go!" George shouted.

Rose and Cowgirl were already climbing into the Hummer.

Brock said, "So the road actually ends back that way? The way you described it?"

Mounting her motorcycle, Rita said, "See for yourself. We're outta here." Then she cranked up and revved the motor, shutting down further discussion.

Brock and his female companion Miranda climbed back into their van, followed by the dwarf, who had neglected to give his name.

Rose called after him: "Hey, Munchkin! Don't get too close to the edge of the world. You might blow off."

Munchkin gave her the finger, then slammed the van's door. The van turned around and drove off toward the road's end. A minute later, the Hummer was following Rita in the same direction, leaving a reddish dust cloud on the now empty stretch of road.

The sky was noticeably brighter but there was still no sign of the sun through the hazy overcast. Hunched over the steering wheel as if he couldn't see ahead very well, George piloted the Hummer slowly over the cracked and potholed road and through the dust trailing the black van.

"Those fucks never answered your question, Kiddo," Rose said. "Why they came and what they're gonna do here."

"Because you interrupted and talked over them," he said.

"I did?"

"Yep."

"Well, shit. But they did come here on purpose, right? Didn't they say that?"

"Yeah, I think. Something about accepting their fate."

"I don't like it." Rose had a tense chokehold on her rock hammer. "They're not good guys. Goddamn religious freaks. Can't trust dipshits like that. They shouldn't be here."

"Neither should we," Cowgirl said from the front seat.

Kidd shook his head. "I'm not sure I should be anywhere."

"What the fuck does that even mean?" Rose elbowed him.

"*Here* shouldn't be here." He suddenly pointed ahead and said, "There's Rita."

Rita had stopped in the middle of the road, waiting for them, and she signaled them to turn around.

George stopped the vehicle and slowly wheeled around, taking care not to let the vehicle's tires go off-road. "This should be far enough back to get up enough speed," he said. "This has got to work."

Then he gunned the gas and the Hummer shot forward with Rita following on her bike.

"Tally-ho, motherfuckers!" Rose shouted.

CHAPTER TWENTY-SEVEN

The Hummer hit 60 mph at approximately the same place the black van had entered The Big Nowhere. Rose held her breath and gripped the back of the seat in front of her, bracing for any potential impact, though she didn't really expect much of one. She didn't believe it would work. She wasn't entirely ready to leave this place and she didn't think this strange terrain wanted them to leave. Not yet. As much as she didn't want to get torn apart by trocs, she wanted to explore the geological mysteries of this impossible world. They were here for a reason and she was dying to discover it. The trick was to discover it without actually dying. She felt the odds were in her favor. She *hoped* they were in her favor.

"It's not happening," Kidd said. He was sitting to Rose's left, now turning in his seat to look back at Rita.

"Fuck da fuckety fuck!" Rose half-yelled, not because she was disappointed that their exit plan hadn't work but because she wasn't ready to admit to the others that she was sort of happy it hadn't worked.

"Maybe Rita can make it even if we don't," Kidd said. "Come on, come on, hit it. Hit that hole for home!"

Rose looked back through the Hummer's wide rear window and saw the motorcycle's headlight cutting a path through the dust. She realized in that instant that she didn't want to see Rita disappear into that elusive crazy-ass passage back to the familiar world of the 21st century. They needed Rita, needed her beautiful, bold badassery, needed it more than ever now that they were going to be stuck here indefinitely—maybe even permanently. If you needed someone to have your back, Rita was the one. Silently, Rose chanted: *Don't make it, don't make it, don't...*

"Fuck!" Kidd bellowed when it was clear that Rita was still behind them, not on her way back to the land of the free and home of the fucking depraved.

"It's okay, Kidd," she said. "Chill. We *need* her with us. She wouldn't want to desert us. We're a fucking team, remember?"

"But I got her into this. It's on me."

"No, dude, it's not. She wanted to come. She knows what she's doing, which is why it's good that she's still here. Don't you get that?"

The Hummer slowed to a stop. Up front, George and Mallory were arguing about something but Rose wasn't listening to them. She placed a hand on Kidd's thigh, just above the knee. She didn't like what she was seeing on his face or in his eyes. "White Eyes, you still with me?" She squeezed his kneecap hard enough to tweak the nerves bundled there.

"Ow! Yes, I'm with you. Jeez."

"Just making sure."

"So here we are," he said, "stuck on the road to nowhere until the next full moon. Or forever, whichever comes first."

"That almost makes sense," Rose said.

Kidd opened the door on his side and started to get out as Rita rode up and stopped in front of the Hummer.

"Where you going?" Rose asked, grabbing his arm.

"To take a leak."

"I'll come with you. To watch for trocs while you drain the lizard."

"You just want to see my cock." He gave her a crooked grin.

"I wanna make sure one of those flying fuckers doesn't mistake it for a juicy worm and swoop down and snatch it right off."

"You want to hold it for me?"

"Been there, done that." She slid out of the backseat behind him and they walked to the uneven edge of the road. As his piss splattered the ground, Rose scanned the brightening sky for flying demons and also kept her eyes out for trocs on the ground.

A minute went by and Kidd was still at it. He shivered in the chill air.

"Damn, dude, you piss like a fucking racehorse."

"Yeah, well…"

Rita cut her engine, dismounted, looked at Kidd and said, "Perfect picture of our predicament, Kidd. We're all stuck here with our dicks in our hands."

He made a sound that might've been a laugh. Finally his stream slowed to a trickle, then he shook himself off several times and zipped up. Rose was turning back to the vehicle when she saw a dark shape hurtling from the sky, a flash of indigo, and then the robed body hit the ground three feet in front of her with a loud thud and a hollow pop. The pop was the man's skull cracking open against the rocks.

It had happened so fast that neither Rose nor Kidd had time to react. They wide-eyed "cult leader" Brock's lifeless body as the flying demon that had dropped it gained altitude, soaring off into the purpling sky.

Rita had her pistol trained on the shrinking creature but didn't fire.

"Why didn't you shoot that motherfucker?" Rose asked.

Rita dropped her gun in its holster. "Waste of ammo. It was no threat to us. And I might've missed. We have to save our shots for when they come at us. And they will."

"It's like it dropped this poor fuck on purpose for us," Rose said, trying to keep her eyes off the blood pool spreading like an obscene halo around the dead man's broken head.

"It did," Kidd said. "It's meant as a message. But I'm not sure what it means."

"Pretty fucking obvious to me," Rita snapped. "It says *you're next.*"

"Not necessarily," Kidd said.

"What, then?" Rita locked eyes with Kidd.

"I don't know. Maybe like when a pet cat leaves a dead bird on your doorstep as a gift, a sign of friendship or respect?"

Rita shook her head but said nothing.

"That does sound a little nuts, dude," Rose said. "You're thinking the flying guys wanna be our friends? Allies against the creepy-crawler trocs? The enemy of my enemy is my friend, huh? Cult-boy Brock here sure as shit got himself unfriended. Nah, I'm not seeing it. For all we know, it might've been trying to take us out with a Brock bomb. Didn't miss me by much."

Kidd said, "You're probably right. Sort of like in Medieval times when soldiers would catapult plague victims into a city under siege."

Rose shot him her best crazy-eyed look. "No, nothing like that. I don't think poor Brock here has the plague."

"No, but the human bomb part, I mean."

Rose sighed in frustration. This was becoming a hit-and-miss conversation. She and her blood brother were not on the same frequency, and it made her doubly doubt that Kidd was all the way back from his trip to Crazy Town. "Yeah, right. Whatever."

"What about the other ones in the van?" This from George, who was looking at Brock's corpse with a pained expression of his own. "The girl and the little guy?" Cowgirl was standing by the Hummer, keeping her distance from the man who fell to earth.

"Munchkin and what's-her-name," Rose said with a nod.

"Miranda," George remembered.

"I think there was somebody else in the van we didn't see," Kidd said.

"Why would you think that?" George asked.

Kidd shrugged. "I dunno, just a feeling. We should go see. They might need help. If they're still alive."

"If they're smart, they stayed in the van," Rose said. "Brock was too full of himself to be smart. Probably got out of the van to preach to the frigging beasts and convert them to his bullshit cult."

"Cult or not, he's dead meat now," George said. "Let's not speak ill of the dead."

"You just called him 'dead meat' and you're telling *me* not to speak ill?"

Kidd said, "I hate to bring this up but…our food supply is limited and we don't know how long we're going to be here. You think, I mean, uh, should we consider…cooking and eating him?"

Rose: "Dude!"

George: "*What?* Are you *serious?*"

Mallory: "Oh my God, I can't believe you just said that!"

"I don't like the idea of going cannibal either but don't we have to at least consider it?" Kidd threw up his hands when nobody answered. "Okay, okay, we can hash it out later. Right now we should go check on the van people. We might need them. And their van."

"We're not eating *them* either," Rose said, eyeing Kidd with mounting suspicion.

"Mount up and let's ride," George said with cringe-worthy bravado.

Rita had already forked her legs over her bike. She said, "I'm way ahead of you, Kemo Sabe."

CHAPTER TWENTY-EIGHT

The van sat sideways across the broken road. The left rear tire was shredded flat. The doors were shut. No one was visible behind the tinted windows.

Rita rolled to a stop beside the driver's door and rapped her pistol on the window. The Hummer pulled up behind the van's rear end.

The van's window powered halfway down and the blond woman called Miranda stuck her face in the opening and said, "Thank God. Are they gone?"

"Those flying fuckers, yeah, they're gone. They dropped your guy Brock on us and he's gone too. Why the hell didn't he stay in the van?"

"But those others," Miranda said. "On the ground. That flattened our tire?"

Rita said, "Those road-running assholes, right. I don't see any but that doesn't mean they're not around."

"God, it was terrible. The way it swooped down and knocked Brock flat. Then it sat on him like a vulture or something worse and started ripping into him." Miranda's big eyes brimmed with tears and her voice warbled with emotion. "I can still hear his screams. Then he... went quiet and the thing picked him up and flew off with Brock just... just hanging like a broken doll."

"And then it dropped him almost on top of us," Rita said.

"He...he's dead, right?" Miranda's eyes got bigger as if they were trying to hold back a torrent of tears.

"What do you *think*? Sure he's dead." Rita looked back at the shredded tire. "I hope you've got a spare for that flat."

From the van's passenger seat, the dwarf said, "Of course we do. We're not stupid."

"Then why aren't you changing the fucking tire instead of just sitting here with your dick in your hand?"

"Coz I don't wanna get snatched up like Brock did. And my penis is *not* in my hand."

"Get your ass out of there and change the tire," Rita said without raising her voice. "We'll cover you. I don't suppose you cult kooks have guns."

Miranda drew back as if slapped. "We're not a cult. We're seekers." Then she added, "Seekers on the path."

"Looks like you took the wrong fucking road, darling," Rita scoffed. Then she summoned Rose and Kidd and told them to stand ready with their weapons for possible threats from the ground. She would watch the skies for any aerial attacks. George and Cowgirl remained in the Hummer, which was where Rita preferred they stay for now. The fewer folks on the ground, the less she would have to worry about. She did not want to see anybody else get ripped apart or carried away.

But the little guy in the passenger seat was not ready to leave off defending his religious beliefs. "This most certainly is the right road," he insisted, raising his voice so it would carry outside the van. "This is an Annunaki road. But you have no idea who the Annunaki are, I'm sure."

Rose caught some of what the dwarf was saying and she said, "Wrong, Munchkin, I know about the Annunaki. They're reptilian gods. Or aliens from another dimension. You think that's what the trocs are? Don't tell me you came here to worship these lizard fuckers."

"Jesus Christ!" Rita shouted. "Everybody shut the fuck up and let's get this tire changed!"

The little man got out of the vehicle, muttering under his breath. After several clumsy attempts, he managed to get the jack in place and jacked up the rear. His small hands shook as he began to loosen the lug nuts.

"Damn, Munch," Rose said, "I thought you said you knew how to do this. You shoulda loosened the lug nuts first."

"My name's not Munch. And it's not Munchkin. It's Nacho."

"No way your name's Nacho."

"The fuck it ain't," he said as he removed the first nut. "*Ignacio Silva, nickname Nacho.*"

"No shit," Rose said. "Well fuck me, Nacho."

"No thanks."

Rose couldn't help herself. She gave him and crooked grin and said, "Nacho cupa tea, eh?"

Rita yelled, "Jesus fucking Christ! Cut the shit and hurry the fuck up. This ain't a high school field trip."

Rita's angry remarks echoed in the rocky hollows and crevasses. This alien landscape worked weirdly well as an echo chamber. The echoes had echoes and took an unnaturally long time to trail off and die into silence.

Rose caught Miranda's eye and said, "Well, do you? Have guns?"

"No, of course not," Miranda said. "Why would we?"

Just then, Rita noticed a sudden shift—the crazed look in Kidd's eyes—and now he was bringing his gun around in her direction. Was he so fucked in the head that he thought he had to shoot *her*? In the split second she had to decide if she needed to shoot him first, in self-defense, the track of his eyes went past her so that he was looking behind her, over her shoulder, and he fired. She ducked and twisted around in time to see the troc fall a few feet behind her. Its eyes immediately glazed and turned milky in death.

"Troc-a-doodle-doo," Kidd said to his kill.

"Christ, Kidd," Rita said, "for a second there I thought you were gonna shoot me. I almost shot you. We need to get the fuck out of this place. Some-fucking-how. Sooner the better."

Miranda said, "You sure say the f-word a lot."

"Fuck you, 'Randa," Rita said.

Miranda put her window up and looked away.

Rose addressed Nacho: "Hey, fuck-nut, hurry up with those lug nuts, Nacho dude."

Without looking up from his task, he said, "Bite me, bitch."

"Take that stupid bathrobe off and you'd get it done a lot faster," Rose needled Nacho.

He gave her a deadpan look as he ceased his nut-tightening work. "It's a cloak, not a bathrobe, you idiot."

Rita took two long strides toward him and jammed the muzzle of her pistol against his head. "Not another word before that tire is ready to roll or your brain gets a blowout."

Rose snickered but dropped her verbal sparring with the dwarf. The little guy had a quick temper and she didn't want to provoke him to further insults with Rita's gun to his head. Rose was taking a liking to Nacho and didn't want to get him killed. Rita stepped back from the dwarf to give him room to work.

Kidd stood stiffly over the troc he'd just shot, reminding Rose of a predator guarding its kill.

Nacho rose to his full height (which couldn't have been more than 4 feet) held up the lug wrench in his right hand and said, "Can I talk now without getting shot?"

Rita stopped pointing her pistol at him but kept it out and ready in case another troc attack was forthcoming. "Your flat's fixed," she said, "we're out of here." Pause. "You're welcome."

"Yeah, thanks," Nacho said.

Rita touched Kidd's arm. "You OK?"

Kidd looked at her with empty eyes but he nodded.

"So where do you guys go from here?" Rose asked the dwarf. "I mean, like you came to this fucked up place deliberately, right? You meant to be here. Here it is and that's all it is, the Big Nowhere. So now what? You know how to get back to the real world?"

Nacho's face twitched into a worried scrunch. "Brock did. Or thought he did. Now we're fucked. Unless you assholes know how to get back."

Rose shook her head. "We don't but we're still looking. We should stick together. You guys follow us. Safety in numbers, like."

Rita revved her bike.

"OK if I ride with you guys?" Rose asked.

"Yeah, sure. Why not?"

Rose shouted to Rita that she was going to ride in the van. Rita shrugged, then signaled to George to turn the Hummer around and move out.

Rose climbed into the van with Nacho the Munchkin. "So tell me what you know about the Annunaki."

CHAPTER TWENTY-NINE

Kidd settled into the Hummer's backseat and wondered if his companions could see that he was wearing someone else's face. Or maybe he wasn't really but his face didn't feel like his own. It was changing, morphing into something foreign, something entirely alien to him. And it wasn't just his face. It was as if he were wearing another person's skin. He touched the scar under his eye. Was it bigger? Rougher to the touch? Growing? Would the damned thing consume him completely? What a crazy idea! And here came another one: Like the man in Kafka's "The Metamorphosis" who wakes up changed into a big bug, Kidd was going to become just one big scar in the shape of a man. Insane! Absolutely fucking nuts. And yet, here he was, right where he was supposed to be, in this impossible world, answering his calling. His totem-mark scar had called him—had been calling him for years—here to meet his dubious destiny. Fighting it was pointless. It was not a fight he could hope to win.

He was hardening, inside and out, crusting over, organs turning brittle, his mind hardening toward to a new breaking point. Soon he could become part of this eerie terrain of jagged rocks and dusty stones, his body absorbed by the desolate land, his soul annexed by this heartless uncharted realm.

But then a different sort of hardening asserted itself. Hardening born of a deep aching desire, raw blood-red lust. Was that a boner in his pants or was he just happy to be out of his mind? He laughed to himself.

*   *   *

Rose listened as Nacho told her what he knew about the Annunaki. Miranda drove the van, staying right on the Hummer's bumper for fear of getting left behind.

"It's the Lizard Apocalypse, no shit," he said. "Of course, that's crazy conspiracy theory crap, right? Fantasy and science fiction nonsense. Robert E. Howard—the guy that came up with that Conan the Barbarian crap?—first exposed our 'lizard overlords' in a story he wrote nearly a hundred years ago. Reality disguised as fiction? Reptilian shape-shifters from outer space running the entire world? Gimme a fucking break, right? Annunaki illuminati. Come on."

"So you're not buying it. What about your boy Brock? He seemed pretty fucking serious about it."

"And look where that got him. These fucking lizard things are real, no doubt, and maybe they rule the roost in this fucked up world here but no way are they secretly running things back in our world." Nacho put his hand on Rose's knee. "Look, we are not a cult. We're musicians, a fucking heavy metal band. We *were*. We were trying to get Brock's head out of his ass so we could pull off a comeback, you know, get the band together again, cut a new album, but he couldn't let go of this End of the Road alternate dimension bullshit. Who the fuck knew it would turn out to be true? We thought we were just humoring him, playing along to let him see that none of it was real. But here the fuck we are and it's too fucking real. But Brock's dead and I just want to get the fuck out of here before lizard motherfuckers come back for my tender ass."

"You're a metal band, no shit?" Rose was having a hard time getting past this unexpected revelation.

"Yeah, maybe you heard of us. Satan's Butt Plugz. Plugs with a *z* instead of an *s*."

"Uh, no I'm pretty sure I would've remembered that name," she said, trying to keep from laughing and hurting the little dude's feelings. But *Satan's Butt Plugz*?

"We were like Five Finger Death Punch by way of Goatwhore, extreme ripping shit."

A deep voice exploded from the back of the van: "My ass! Five Finger Death Punch couldn't punch my dick. They're fake metal. Don't listen to Nacho. Who the fuck *are* you anyway?"

A guy with thick golden hair covering his shoulders like a luxurious cape sat straight up in his seat and bore into Rose with eyes that seemed to glow with a furtive inner fire.

"I'm…Rocky." Everything about the man made her feel very small and childlike.

"You don't sound too sure," he said, squaring his massive shoulders and rolling his head on his neck to work out some stiffness.

"Sometimes I'm Rose." Overcoming her shock (if that's what it was), she shot back: "Who the fuck're you?"

The van's dim interior seemed to brighten as the guy leaned forward, a halo of golden light around his big head. His long braided goatee made him resemble a Viking.

He made a deep rumbling noise that might've been a growl.

Nacho said, "That's Zip. Zip Gunn."

This time she couldn't stop herself from laughing. Nacho shook his head as if warning her—too late—not to laugh at the ridiculous name. But how could she not? This big hunk of manliness nicknamed after a half-ass handgun, homemade with a pipe and rubber band?

Zip Gunn stood up but the van hit a bump or a crack in the road and his hulking bulk dropped back onto the seat. He grabbed the seatback in front of him and pulled himself back up. "Zack Gunn, Zachary in fact. My band name is Zip Gunn."

"'Sup, Zip? You know how we can get the hell out of this place and get back home?"

"Da fuck would I know that?" Zip shrugged. "I just fucking got here."

"So go back the way you came while maybe the way is still open. And we'll follow you out. And if it doesn't work, then you can slay those lizard fucks with ear-splitting heavy metal."

"We don't have our gear with us," Nacho said as if she were crazy. "It's not like we're on tour, ya know."

"That was a joke, Nutso," Rose said with a wink.

"Funny cunt," he said.

"Whoa, little fella," Zip said as if addressing a disobedient pup.

"You don't talk like that to a lady."

"Lady my ass," the dwarf sniped.

"You wish," Rose returned fire.

Nacho muttered to himself.

The van began to weave along the road, the right wheels pounded by what passed for the road's shoulder.

Zip shouted: "Hey! Miranda, what the fuck? Are you drunk?"

Miranda said, "Sorry, sorry. I must've dozed off."

Rose wondered how anyone could doze off in this place, under these circumstances, but she didn't voice this thought. She began to regret her decision to ride with these strangers, these metalhead poseurs, or whatever they were. But there was something about little Nacho that drew her to him. He was grumpy as shit but he made it somehow cute. It wasn't a sexual thing, at least she didn't think so. But she did wonder what it would be like banging him. Did he have a dwarf dick? Was that even a thing? For all she knew he could be hung like the proverbial horse. She chuckled at the image. *My little pony!*

"What's so fucking funny?" Nacho snapped.

"Ah, nothing. Just can't believe how crazy this shit is. Like, you know, how can this even be possible? Riding with a washed-up metal band at the End of the Road. Or end of the world, whichever comes first."

"We're not washed-up," Zip said as he slid his bulk into the seat behind them. "Washed-out maybe but not washed-up. Replacing Brock will be a problem. He did most of the vocals."

He ran his fingers through Rose's hair. Rose jerked away.

"Hey, take it easy," Zip said. "I'm not gonna hurt you. I like your look. Tomboy chic. You a lesbian?"

"What? No! I'm a rock hound, not a pussy hound."

"A what? A cock hound?"

"*Rock.* I'm a geologist. Nicknamed Rocky, get it?"

"Rocky Rose, yeah sure, I get it," Zip said. "I got a rock you can ride. If you can handle it."

"Fuck you, Zipper Man. I'm not your fucking groupie. I think Nacho here is more my speed."

Nacho looked at her with his mouth agape.

Zip Gunn laughed. A surprisingly high-pitched laugh from such a hulk of a man.

Rose changed the subject. "This is about the time we should be phasing back to the normal world if this shit's gonna work. I'm not getting a good vibe. I might be stuck here with you cray-cray fucks."

From behind the wheel Miranda shouted: "They're going too fast, I can't keep up!"

"Oh Jesus, those things are chasing them!" This from Nacho, who'd jumped up for a better view of the Hummer's bumper in the van's bouncing headlights.

Rose saw two trocs, one on each side of the Hummer, and then there was a third and a fourth joining the chase. All but one of them raced along on all fours, the odd one lopping upright on two legs. "Here we go again," she said with a sinking sigh.

Kidd saw them out there, running alongside the vehicle with a sleek grace he could only admire and even envy. They were, in their own unearthly way, beautiful. Creatures entirely alien to him and yet somehow they were his kin. Weren't they? He longed to be out there right now, running with them, running with the pack—no, not *pack*, what was the word? *Lounge.* A lounge of lizards, yeah. He remembered that from zoology class taught by that science department wonk with the wacky bowties and the Coke-bottle glasses. Mr. Denton. *Doctor Denton* they called him behind his back because he was a man of small stature and you could easily picture him in a pair of those Dr. Denton footed sleepers. If he were here to see these badass lizard beasts, then old Dr. Denton would shit his ridiculous jammies. These monsters were truly awesome. And fast.

Kidd saw what they were up to, saw their attack formation and discerned their strategy. If it worked, then Kidd and his companions would be meeting these creatures up close and personal, face to snout, very soon.

"Shoot 'em out the window, Kidd!" George yelled. "Keep 'em off the tires. Two flats and we're fucked!"

Kidd realized he still had the pistol in his hand and he raised it up to eyelevel but he no longer wanted to shoot these trocs. *His* trocs. Something in his blood was singing out to them, as their blood sang out to his, an uncanny harmony happening. Unlikely though it was, it *was*.

Then a staggered series of fateful events began. Two loud pops, one almost on top of the other, thudded the undercarriage as the attackers punctured tires on both sides. The Hummer bumped from side to side over the road and immediately lost speed. The driver's-side window imploded, glass and the head, shoulders and claws of a troc converging on the left side of George's face and head. Mallory screamed. A gunshot concussed the air and made Kidd's ears ring as shrilly as a fire alarm. The troc hooked its claws in George and sank its teeth in his neck as the Hummer veered left and ran off-road, banging onto the treacherous terrain, bumping and juddering and going up on two wheels and then tipping over and finally crashing with a booming THWANG!

The world went insanely topsy-turvy and it took Kidd along. Mallory was no longer screaming. She had come to rest on top of her husband, who in turn had come to rest on the dead troc partially crushed beneath the Hummer's left side. The vehicle's engine died.

Mallory's neck was twisted at such a hideous angle that Kidd had to hope she had died instantly and wasn't still alive to suffer. But he had his own ass to worry about and now his ass was on the line, his butt hanging out the window and the gun no longer in his hand. He tasted blood. Salty and unusually sweet on his tongue.

Talon-like claws sank into his right butt cheek as a troc pulled him through the window and out of the vehicle. The pain was sweet, exciting. His boner swelled. Raised its horny head against his trousers. Whatever was next to happen, he knew he couldn't fight it. It was meant to be, the deal long ago sealed with the flick of a claw and the drawing of his blood.

Miranda hit the brakes and the van lurched to a stop where the Hummer had run off the road and flipped over on its side. Rose was frozen to her seat, unable to move until she saw the troc grab Kidd and pull him out of the wreckage. Then she was up and out of the van with the gun in her hand, ready to plug the pebbly fucker and save her blood brother. Nacho shouted after her: "Get back in the van!"

Rita rode up and hopped off her bike, brandishing her pistol in pissed off way like she didn't have time for this fucking troc shit.

Rose was relieved that she wouldn't have to risk hitting Kidd with a wild shot. Rita would handle it with her expert marksmanship. "Don't hit Kidd!" Rose needlessly shouted.

Rita stopped an arm's length away from where Kidd and the troc were grappling on the ground and shouted, "Let go of it, Kidd, so I can get a clear shot!"

But Kidd didn't let go. To Rose they looked like lovers desperately embracing, driven by unnatural lust. The creature shredded Kidd's pants and they fell away, revealing his huge erection.

Rita yelled, "Goddammit, Kidd!"

Beneath the tatters of his shirt Rose saw greenish, pebbled skin. She thought her eyes must be playing tricks, or that he and the troc were so intimately entwined that she mistook the troc's skin for his. But no. Kidd's legs and his bare ass *had* taken on the appearance of lizard-like skin. *What the fuck?* Was Kidd becoming a were-troc? *No way.*

Rita bent down and aimed her pistol just inches from the troc's head. Before she could pull the trigger, another troc leapt at her and took her to the ground.

"Jesus fuck!" This from Zip Gunn, who had exited the van and was now rushing past Rose to join the fray. His golden hair billowing behind him like cape of royalty, he grabbed the monster and yanked it off of Rita, raised it high over his head and body-slammed the beast to the road in a move worthy of the WWE Raw wrestlers she used to watch for laughs. Then he stomped the thing's head to skullish mush with his size-12 engineer motorcycle boots.

Things were happening so fast that Rose could hardly follow all the action. Mallory fell out of the Hummer, one arm dangling limply at her side, her head hanging to one side in an odd disturbing angle, her face and neck ripped with bloody wounds, her lower lip simply gone. She staggered several feet and then fell on her ruined face. Rose made no move to go to her, to help. The woman was beyond help.

Rita sat up but stayed down. She didn't appeared to be bleeding but she had a dazed look on her face.

And what the fuck was Kidd doing? Rose was seeing it but not believing it. *No fucking way.* But she *was* seeing it. Kidd was fucking the troc. He had his dick in the thing's backside, in one hole or another, pumping and humping away at the lizard-skinned fucker.

"What's wrong with you?" Rose shouted. "Get your dick out of that thing! Are you nuts?"

But of course he was. *Fucking* nuts! He wasn't himself. He wasn't even human anymore. He was Lizard Man. And the world had gone completely insane, around the bend and into The Big Nowhere, never to return.

CHAPTER THIRTY

"Dude!" Zip Gunn bellowed at Kidd. "What the fuck?"

Kidd continued to hump the troc. The troc didn't seem to mind. Rose wasn't sure if it was humping back or if Kidd was providing all the thrust. Of all the shocking things she had experienced in this place, Kidd's impromptu bestiality was the worst, most alarming. She wanted to look away but she couldn't tear her eyes off the perverted spectacle.

Zip Gunn hovered indecisively over Kidd and the troc, as if he might be considering stomping both their skulls. At this point, Rose wasn't sure if that was a bad idea, given Kidd's frighteningly fast metamorphosis. If her blood brother was still residing within that freaky body, she couldn't feel him, couldn't detect any familiar vibe of human presence. She feared he had already checked out, mind, body and soul.

"What's *wrong* with this guy?" Zip asked Rose. "He one of yours?"

"Yes. I don't know. He's mine, I mean. I don't know what's happening to him. Looks like he's turning into one of them. But how's that even possible?"

"I don't think impossible lives here." He shook his head in disgust. "I gotta stop this shit. It just ain't right." He kicked the troc in the head so hard that it dislodged the beast from Kidd's desperate grasp. Kidd's penis popped out bloody.

"Oh my God!" Rose hoped it wasn't Kidd's blood. She didn't think it was. What made more (but not much more) sense was that the troc was a virgin until Kidd broke her cherry. But if these things were like lizards, the female had no vagina. She had a cloaca—one hole for shitting, pissing and reproduction. Which probably meant they weren't like lizards except for their skin.

The troc lay lifeless next to a stunned Kidd. Zip Gunn brought his boot down hard on the beast's head again and again until its brains and cranium were crushed to purple pulpy mush. Rose had to look away from the gruesome pulverization. Her eyes went back to Kidd—or whatever he'd become—and settled on the pebbled skin of his bloody penis. *Troc cock! On my bloody brother.* Could she still reach him? Was there enough of him in that fucked-up head of his? Would he turn on her, try to rip her apart or rape her? *My God, will I have to shoot him?*

Miranda sat behind the wheel of the idling van, watching the bizarre scene play out on the other side of the windscreen's dirty glass. Her hands tightened on the steering wheel. How could any of this be real? Was she dreaming? Sitting in a car at some virtual drive-in theater with a gritty monster movie playing in front of her eyes? Wishful thinking! This was real and she couldn't just sit and do nothing. Panic rising inside her, she knew she had to act to escape it. A passive position was untenable in this impossible place, this hidden hell on earth.

She goosed the gas and gunned the engine, then took her foot off the brake.

It had been hibernating within him for years and now it was awake, supplanting his consciousness with its own perceptions, alienating him from himself—his old self, which was flickering, guttering in bizarre winds, soon to be extinguished forever. Inserting himself into the female had felt like homecoming to a place he'd never called home, had never even been.

The roar of a badly tuned engine caught his attention and he looked up to see the frontend of the van charging at him like giant beast with its grill-mouth open and hungry, headlights glaring like fierce eyes. Rose yelled and ducked out of the path of the accelerating vehicle but Kidd didn't move. He felt no fear. Whatever happened was suppose to happen. If this was the way it was to end for him, so be it.

As he was opening his arms to welcome his fate, the 3,000-pound vehicle struck him dead-on and knocked him flat on his back. The van passed over him like a dark leviathan swimming over a deep-sea diver. Then numbing darkness swallowed him.

Rose saw it happen but she could hardly believe what she was seeing. Miranda ran Kidd down, ran *over* him and crashed into the overturned Hummer, and then a wide patch of rocky ground beneath both vehicles collapsed and took them down. Rita teetered on the edge of the big sinkhole and Zip grabbed her and pulled her to safety. She stumbled into his arms as if into the embrace of a long-lost lover.

Rose's impulse was to run to the hole and see if Nacho and Miranda could be somehow be rescued from the sunken van but she wasn't certain the ground was stable, and she didn't want to join them down in the hole. The thing might still be hungry. She approached cautiously, stepping lightly.

"Look at that," Zip said in an excited voice as he pointed into the sinkhole. "Are you seeing that? Holy crow! That's…"

"A flying fucking saucer," Rita said. "A crashed UFO?"

Rose got as close as she dared to the edge and looked down. The Hummer and the van had fallen roughly twenty feet down and had come to rest on what sure as shit looked like a spacecraft straight out of a steampunk fantasy. It had the appearance of tarnished bronze with odd industrial-looking nobs and ornate fixtures spaced at intervals along its surface. With the two vehicles on top of it and with part of the craft embedded in the earth, she couldn't tell how big the thing was but she guessed it must be at least 40 feet in diameter.

She couldn't see Kidd and figured he must be under the van. There wasn't much light in the sinkhole and she couldn't see inside the van to see if Nacho and Miranda were injured from the drop.

"We have to get them out of there," Rose said, looking to Rita and Zip.

"How the fuck can we do that?" Rita said.

Zip shouted, "Miranda! Are you OK?"

No answer.

Then he tried: "Nacho! Answer me you little shit!"

No response.

"There's a rope in the hummer," Rose remembered. "We could pull 'em up one at a time."

"So one of us has to drop down there to do it," Rita said, shaking her head.

"I'll go," Rose said. "I'm the lightest. And we need Zip's big ass up here to muscle them up."

"Then hurry the fuck up," Rita snapped. "I ain't waiting around to get attacked again by one of your troc motherfuckers."

"Watch your backs," Rose told them. "If they get both of you guys, I'll die down in that hole."

"That's a pretty steep drop," Zip observed. "Hope you don't break your legs."

Rose sat on the rim of the sinkhole with her feet dangling. She tried to slow her breathing and calm her sudden fear of putting herself deeper in danger.

"Not getting cold feet, are you?" Zip goaded.

"Fuck you," she said and then pushed off and dropped down.

Sharp pain seared her left ankle when she landed on the assumed saucer. She fell back onto the seat of her pants and instinctively grabbed her injured ankle. "Sonofabitch!" she hissed at the pain as if that would make it go away.

"You all right?" Zip called down, his voice echoing within the earthen confines of the hole.

Rose gently flexed the ankle. Rubbed it again. "I don't think it's broken. Just a sprain. I think."

"Can you walk on it?" Rita asked.

She didn't answer. She'd hardly even heard the question. Her attention was momentarily diverted away from her pain and to the inexplicable sensation of warmth on her rear. How could this steampunk saucer be warm? And getting hotter? Hadn't it been buried here in the rocks for who knew how long? Long enough for the earth to cover it over with slow geologic changes. Maybe for many millennia. How could it be threatening to burn her ass now? No clue. But it gave her the impetus to stand up and test her sprained ankle. Her boots could stand the heat better than her butt. And she had a job to do. Nacho and that crazy bitch Miranda.

She reached forward and braced one hand on the van's rear bumper as she stood up. The ankle hurt but she knew she could hobble well enough. She'd sprained this same ankle once before, doing a layup during a high school basketball game. She'd won the game but lost her starting position for several weeks due to the injury.

She pressed her face to the glass of the back window but she couldn't see anything except the seatbacks in the interior dimness. "Nacho! Hey, you all right?" She banged her fist on the window. "Knock, knock, motherfucker!"

Nothing.

"Miranda! Wake up!"

She pounded her fist again, this time on the on the van's rear door.

"Shit," she said, and then tried the door handle. Unlocked, it opened, and she boosted herself into the van. She moved carefully, slowly through the shadowy interior, in no hurry to see what she was afraid she might lay her eyes on. She didn't want to see any more death. Kidd—or whatever he'd become—was surely dead beneath these vehicles. The Fluckers, the others…

A soft moan. A whimper. From the seat behind the driver's seat.

"Nacho? Dude, you all right?"

She looked over the seat's headrest and saw his little body sprawled crossways, seatbelt holding him in place. She couldn't see any blood or outward signs of injury but she knew he might well have internal injuries. Or maybe he was only stunned from the impact with the Hummer and the fall into this huge sinkhole. She reached down, patted his shoulder and called his name again. His eyes fluttered but didn't open.

"Nacho! Wake up. We have to get out of here."

He moaned again. Rose moved past him to see how Miranda had fared. If the bitch was dead, it would serve her right. What the hell had she been thinking? Running over Kidd hadn't been enough; she'd wrecked the only means of transportation out of this place—except for Rita's bike. If there *was* a way out of this damned monster-cursed world. But first Rose had to get out of this hellhole and take Nacho with her. Miranda wouldn't be making it out. She was already dead. Slumped over the steering wheel, her head hanging to one side, neck obviously broken. Rose confirmed that she had no pulse.

When she turned back to Nacho, he had his eyes open but he looked dazed, like he didn't know where he was or how he got here.

"Nacho, get with it, man, we have to get you out of here. Can you walk?"

He looked at her as if he'd never seen her before.

Rose unfastened his seatbelt and gently tugged on his arm to help him stand. He didn't resist. He let himself be led like a bewildered child. He held one hand to his head as if trying to make a fierce headache magically go away or just to keep his head on his shoulders. Rose helped him out of the van and sat him down on the still warming saucer. "Wait here. I've got to get a rope out of the Hummer."

Rita was hyped, ready to rumble if another attack came. And she had this longhaired hulk to help her. He was no Johnny Headstone but he sure as shit knew how to stomp monsters' heads into the ground. "Sing out if you see one, and I'll blow his shit away," she said. "And thanks for getting that one off me. You saved my ass."

He sort of smiled and said, "We make a good team. What you have to do when your ass is on the line. You're a damned good shot with that pistol."

Rose called up from the hole: "I'm throwing the rope to you! Be ready to catch it!"

Zip went to the sinkhole's edge, held his big hands out and said, "Ready."

Rita watched as Rose tossed one end of the rope up into Zip's grasp. The dwarf had the other end of the rope tied under his arms and around his chest.

"Lift him slow and easy," Rose said. "He's still out of it."

"How's Miranda?" Zip asked.

"She's dead."

He didn't visibly react, maintaining his stoic demeanor. He wrapped his end of the rope several times around his wrist and began feed it to the surface. He did it effortlessly, as easily as he might reel in a small fish.

Rita watched the big man pull the little man up and slowly drag him out of the sinkhole. She didn't see the troc until it was almost upon her, sweeping down from the sky like a nightmarish pterodactyl. She got off one shot before it struck her down.

When Rose saw that Nacho was safely out of the hole, a rasping moan drew her attention to Kidd, who was on his feet and leaning against the rear of the van. But the thing wearing Kidd's bloody, tattered clothes wasn't Kidd. Except for the eyes. There was recognition in his eyes. There was pleading in them, as if whatever was left of her old friend in his new Troc Man body was trying desperately to communicate something to her. There was no sense of threat from him. It came to her that being run over by the van had brought him to his senses, had jolted him back into his remaining humanity. His left leg was mangled and bloody, and the way he was bent over suggested that his back might be broken. A mere human couldn't be standing there the way he now was.

"Kidd? Are you—"

He opened his mouth and made a croaking noise that sounded like "You."

Tears came into her eyes. She cried, "I don't know what to do. I don't know how to help you."

She heard the gunshot from the surface but she couldn't take her eyes from Kidd. She figured Rita was finishing off another troc.

Kidd spoke again. Two words this time: "Ep...you."

"Help you?" Rose said. "You mean *help me?*"

His misshapen head slowly nodded.

"How?"

His reptilian face twisted into a countenance unreadable as a human expression. "Om," he mouthed.

"What?"

"Oo *om.*" His eyes opened wider as if he wanted her to look into his head and read the thought in his broken mind.

Then Rose got it. "Home. You want to help me home?"

He nodded. His eyes seemed to light up with that old familiar Billy the Kidd spark.

"Right, okay, but first we have to get out of this hole."

With great effort, he pushed away from the van, straightened his spine and stood nearly erect. Then he reached for Rose. She tried to back away but he had already wrapped his arms around her.

The troc on top of Rita shrieked in her right ear, fluttered its leathery wings as if it had suddenly decided to lift off and fly away. Then the wings folded on its back and greenish fluid leaked from its mouth, splattering her shoulder. The troc convulsed, then went stiff and still. Its body was remarkably lightweight and Rita pushed it off her without much difficulty. The shot she'd fired just before it had struck her must've hit a vital organ.

Lucky shot, Legs, Johnny Headstone whispered.

The numbness in her chest where the creature had struck her was wearing off, replaced by a piercing ache. Her right breast was bloodied where the fucker's talons had punctured her, her leather jacket and shirt were ripped so she could see three holes, each about the size of a quarter. One of the talons had just missed the nipple and she was grateful for that. She figured the puncture wounds would eventually heal and leave scars, but that was better than losing a nipple.

She looked around for the big longhaired guy, ready to give him hell for not helping her fight off that winged fucker, but there he was, wrestling one of the wingless ones. A big one that was getting the better of him. The dazed dwarf was sitting on his ass, futilely fumbling with the rope knotted around his chest.

Rita grabbed up her gun and offered to shoot the fucker he was fighting.

"No," he yelled, "I got him."

She stuck the pistol in her belt and lifted her shirttail to staunch the blood streaming from her breast. It hurt like a bitch but she refused to give in to pain and let pain make *her* its bitch. Instead, she focused mind and will on getting the hell out of this place. She would do it the same way she got here. On her bike. The question was: Who would she take with her?

At first Rose struggled within Kidd's engulfing hug but his grip grew so tight that she could hardly breathe, much less resist. Dark spots flashed before her eyes and she thought she was going to pass out. But then the walls of the sinkhole began to flicker and fade away and she was falling into a dreamlike world far from where she'd just been. There was a small, perfectly round hill with a single giant tree on top of it. The tree was laden with strange red fruit resembling deformed tomatoes dripping juice and spilling white seeds. She intuited that the fruit of the tree had healing properties, and she wanted very much to bite into one to taste of its curative powers. She understood then that Kidd wasn't trying to hurt her. He was trying to help her in a way she couldn't comprehend. But then the tree and the hill flashed out of existence and she was back in the hole, locked in Kidd's powerful arms. She could barely breathe but she managed to wheeze out the words: "Let go of me, Kidd."

He didn't let go. He squeezed harder. The hole's dirt walls again fell away and Rose was falling too, falling into yet another location. Blurred colors gave way to darkness, then crackling flashes of light filled her eyes and a familiar place took shape around her. Now she was on solid ground, standing in the middle of a two-lane blacktop with broken-line white striping down the center. *Back in the real world.*

And then she wasn't. The road flashed out of existence and she was back in the goddam sinkhole, passing out in Kidd Troc's spindly arms.

Rita knew it had to be Rose. She would get Rose out of the ground and on the back of her bike and they would ride the fuck out of this hell on earth.

Fuckin' A, Legs. It's your only shot.

She would have to lie to Zip and say she would try to come back to ferry him out of here too. Otherwise, he might try to commandeer her bike for himself before she and Rose could blow out of here.

"You need help with that?" Zip asked her, pointing at her bare and bloodied tit. "That's a lot of blood."

"No," she said sharply, "it's fine." Then she stepped to the edge of the sinkhole and saw that Kidd (or whatever the hell he'd become) and Rose were locked in what appeared to be a desperate embrace. And then they were gone. Vanished in a hazy flash. "What the fuck? Did you see that?"

"See what?" Zip came to stand beside her.

"They just disappeared. Right in front of my fucking eyes. Gone." Rita stared down at the two wrecked vehicles on top of the crashed saucer.

Nacho's muffled cry turned their heads and they saw a troc on top of him, its teeth tearing the dwarf's throat out, arterial blood jetting several inches in the air. Rita raised the pistol to shoot the beast but before she could get off a shot, two more came hurtling at them.

Zip threw his big body at one of them and they met in midair, then fell to the ground where they grappled furiously. Rita took the second one out with a headshot that landed the dead beast at her feet.

It was too late for Nacho. He was bleeding out. Rita shot the dwarf's killer and it fell dead on top of him, his ugly snout still dripping human's blood.

Zip had his huge hands wrapped around the throat of the one he was wrestling and the thing's lizard eyes bulged with panic. Then Zip snapped its neck and tossed it off him. He got to his feet and saw his former band mate dead, his throat ripped away. In a roaring rage, he grabbed the dead troc off Nacho and body-slammed it to the ground and then kicked its head in for good measure.

"Arggghh, god *damn* it, dude," he said to Nacho's corpse. "This wasn't supposed to happen."

"None of this was supposed to happen," Rita said, already moving toward her bike. "Let's get the fuck out of here. Climb on the back and hold tight."

Johnny Headstone's ghost said what he'd often said to her in life when they were Rebel Riders: *Time to fork and ride, Legs.*

Ignoring the pain of her punctured breast, she forked her legs over the chopper and fired it up. Zip got on behind her, gripped her hips with both hands and the thunderous machine shot them down the black road. And hopefully back to the world.

Rose had never cared for wild carnival rides because she had always been prone to motion sickness. Bumper cars and the merry-go-round were more her speed. The ride she was getting in Kidd Troc's arms was the wildest of her life but she understood that it was her only way out of The Big Nowhere, understood she had to suck it up and *get down with the sickness.* His metamorphosis obviously had given him the troc's ability to jump from one reality to the other, and there was enough humanity left in him to want to see his blood sister safely home. But he was severely injured, his back likely broken, and Rose had no idea what would happen if he died with her in his arms as they careered between worlds. She knew he *was* dying. She could feel his life leaking away. His reality-jumping ability apparently was dying with him. She wasn't ready to die. But it was out of her hands now. Wasn't it?

With the earthen scent of the sinkhole still in her nostrils, she rode the Kidd Troc Express to wherever the fuck he was taking her next, the sinkhole left behind them in a blur of dirt and light and sound, a low-pitched hum she could still feel in her belly even after it became inaudible. The tiny hairs on her arms and neck stood up, magnetized by crackling static electricity. She smelled ozone or something like it. *I'm smelling electricity.*

She wanted to thank Kidd for trying mightily to get her back home but she didn't believe she could make sounds between worlds. She wasn't even sure if she was actually breathing. Darkness and light interplayed a soundless duet as they sped along the edge of the abyss, heading, she felt sure, for an end of the line.

The road appeared in a rush and they tumbled to the dark pavement, hitting hard and knocked breathless. Kidd took the brunt of the direct impact with the road, holding her protectively in his Troc Man's arms.

Only now did he relinquish his embrace. He emitted a raspy moan. Rose tried to catch her breath. The air was crisp and cool, with an autumn tang. The sky was overcast. If the sun was up there, she couldn't see it. Still, this had to be home. A manmade blacktop, weeds and grass along the sides of the road. Trees in the distance. Good old U.S. of A.

His arms went slack, then dropped away. Rose rolled off him and got shakily to her feet. He made a sound like air hissing from a punctured tire as blood trickled from his lipless mouth. He convulsed, his head thumping the pavement and his spindly legs kicking as if they wanted to cock up and grasshopper him away in a leap fantastic enough to take him back to the Big Nowhere, anywhere but here where he was surely dying. After what seemed like a full minute of cruel convulsions, he fell still.

Rose knelt down beside him. "*Kidd.* Kidd, I'm so sorry this happened to you. Can you hear me? It's *me*, your old pal Rose. You're my blood brother, my best friend and I…I love you, asshole. You hear me, goddammit?"

His eerie green pupils rolled up and out of sight, his yellowish whites resembling unfinished doll's eyes.

"I love you," she repeated, this time as a hopeless whisper.

She heard a car approaching so she took him by the legs and dragged him out of the road and onto the weed-choked shoulder. A big-ass flame-red Ram pickup with a guy in a cowboy hat behind the wheel zoomed past, its slipstream roughly buffeting her. It felt right. Getting roughed up by a passing vehicle was a fitting end to this fucked-up adventure, a reminder that the world could buffet the fuck out of you and all you could do was try to stand up to it and not get run down or run over. Or lose your best friend. Or turned into a fucking monster and killed for your troubles.

"I would bury you if I had a fucking shovel," she said, crying tearfully now. "I can't just leave you here looking like you do. No offense, you know? Fuck me, I'm babbling. I—"

She heard a distant yet familiar sound. She looked down the road in the direction of the sound. And there it was.

A motorcycle coming on fast. She knew it was Rita even before she could make out her features. She *knew* it. Felt it. It had to be.

Rose stepped to the middle of the blacktop and waved her arms over her head. The bike bore down on her, not slowing. Rose walked toward the bike, still waving, challenging.

Her breast filled with pride at the sight: Rita the badass rebel rider, fearless warrior woman who defeated the monsters on their home turf and fought her way back home.

Rose broke into a big grin as the bike slowed because that meant Rita must've recognized the crazy woman waving like a maniac in the middle of the road. And there was Zip fucking Gunn riding bitch on the back.

Rita rolled to a stop on the side of the road. She remained mounted, engine idling. She shouted to be heard over the rumble: "How the hell did you get here?"

"Kidd Troc magic."

"What?"

"You saw what he turned into. But he's still in there, sort of. But he won't be for long."

"What the fuck are you talking about?"

"Never mind. You better find the nearest hospital, your boob looks pretty bad."

"There's one down this way." Rita nodded at the road ahead. "Get on the back and we'll put all this shit behind us."

"No, you go ahead. I can hitch. I don't want to leave Kidd until he's...gone."

"Honey, that thing ain't Kidd. Kidd's already gone."

Rose saw no point in arguing. She waved them on.

Rita and Zip roared off down the blacktop. Rose watched them until the distance ate them. Then she went back to where Kidd Troc lay dying.

Was he already dead? She thought he was until she saw the slight movement of his chest heaving up and down. He was still breathing. Barely. His eyes blinked, lizard-skin eyelids revealing that his pupils were back. They seemed to search for her. Found her. Focused on her face. Was that pleading in them? A tear ran from the corner of his right eye.

"Kidd. I have to let you go." Tears flooded her eyes and blurred her vision. "I know you understand. You'd do the same for me. I know you would."

She pulled the rock hammer from her belt. Her hand shook. Her voice shook as she said, "I love you, brother. Go in peace."

She raised the hammer and brought it down hard in the center of his greenish forehead, the sharp pick end piercing the skull. The hollow-melon thump it made sickened her as blood gushed from the wound. His eyes bulged, nearly bursting from their sockets.

Rose yanked the pick out of his head, flipped the handle and struck again, this time with the flat head—the one she'd used countless times to break all manner of rocks. She bashed him three more times in rapid succession, desperate to stop his brain functioning and end his suffering.

When she was done, she was covered in his blood but she hardly felt it. She sobbed, she bawled, she mouthed senseless sounds that even she didn't understand.

She couldn't bear to look at the mess she'd made of his head and freaky face, but she could not look away. She leaned forward and buried her face in his alien chest. She cried until she had no more tears.

Thunder rolled and tumbled and shook the ground and rattled her teeth. A light rain was falling. She raised her face to the storm-dark sky. Rain came down harder, washing blood from her face. She didn't move for a long time.

Finally she got to her feet, stuck the hammer in her belt and walked away without another glance at what had once been her best friend. Her blood brother.

She stepped to the road. Stood on the middle of it, half hoping a car or truck would come barreling along and smash into her. She started walking. She listened to the rain splattering the pavement and emptied her head of all else.

The world once again opened to her, inviting her to explore more of its bizarre mysteries. She wasn't sure where she was going, but that was all right. All roads had to lead somewhere.

RANDY CHANDLER is the author of the novels *Dime Detective, Daemon of the Dark Wood, HELLz BELLz,* and the fantasy novel *Angel Steel.* He also co-authored *Duet For the Devil* with t. Winter-Damon (God rest his soul). Randy's collection of short stories is *Devils, Death & Dark Wonders.* He is the Associate Editor of Red Room Press and co-editor of *Year's Best Hardcore Horror.*

Randy has been an indie magazine editor/publisher, a freelance book reviewer, a mental health worker, a gas-pump jockey, an ambulance attendant, a soldier in Vietnam, and a funeral home flunky. He often haunts fields of carnage where angels and devils do battle.

www.ingramcontent.com/pod-product-compliance
Lightning Source LLC
Chambersburg PA
CBHW070928250626
47159CB00009B/3162